CW00920570

THRONEWORLD

THE BEAST ARISES

Discover the latest books in this multi-volume series at
blacklibrary.com

THE BEAST ARISES

BOOK FIVE

THRONEWORLD

GUY HALEY

BLACK LIBRARY

A BLACK LIBRARY PUBLICATION

First published in Great Britain in 2016 by
Black Library
Games Workshop Ltd
Willow Road
Nottingham NG7 2WS UK

10 9 8 7 6 5 4 3 2 1

Produced by Games Workshop in Nottingham

A CIP record for this book is available from the British Library.

UK ISBN 13: 978 1 78496 136 7
US ISBN 13: 978 1 78496 167 1

See Black Library on the internet at
blacklibrary.com

Find out more about Games Workshop
and the world of Warhammer 40,000 at
games-workshop.com

Printed and bound in China

Fire sputters...
The shame of our deaths
and our heresies is done. They are
behind us, like wretched phantoms. This
is a new age, a strong age, an age of Imperium.
Despite our losses, despite the fallen sons, despite the
eternal silence of the Emperor, now watching over us in
spirit instead of in person, we will endure. There will be no
more war on such a perilous scale. There will be an end
to wanton destruction. Yes, foes will come and
enemies will arise. Our security will be
threatened, but we will be ready, our
mighty fists raised. There will be no
great war to challenge us now.
We will not be brought
to the brink like that
again...

ONE

The Last Wall gathers

An armada of slab-sided warships glided in geosynchronous orbit a thousand kilometres over Phall's equator, diverse heraldries proclaiming their masters. Bleached by harsh sunlight unfiltered by atmosphere, the yellow and silver, black, blue, crimson, white and grey of each Space Marine Chapter was nevertheless clear, defiant of the star's glare. Void-deep shadow cut mysterious shapes onto the towering superstructures high on the ships' spines. A million lights shone from their flanks. The craft were larger than cities; thousands dwelled within them, living out lives devoted to war. Great gun maws issued silent challenges to the fathomless interplanetary night. Hangar bays were black slots glimmering with coherence fields, ready to launch the vengeance of the Emperor at the foes of the Imperium.

Still Koorland feared it would not be enough. He counted and recounted the ships, calculating the combined strength of arms arrayed above the world. Ship tonnage, munition payloads, fighter groups, armed bondsmen, serfs and ship

crews, all of it, not only the number of Adeptus Astartes, although they were the group he counted and recounted the most. Each time the mathematics of war came up short. The greatest number of Space Marines gathered in one place since the time of the Scouring, and still it was pitiful in the face of the orkish threat.

'Truly, it is a sight to stir the hearts of men.'

'It is, Brother Issachar,' said Koorland. He moved away from the window to greet the Chapter Master of the Excoriators as he entered the observation deck. The mark of their shared heritage was clear to see – the fist that adorned Issachar's dull white pauldron was the same as that upon Koorland's yellow armour – but it was a kinship sundered. The ways of the sons of Dorn had diverged. Issachar's fist was red, not black, and gripped in its fingers a doubled lightning bolt of yellow that Koorland's lacked. The Excoriator's armour was a mess of nicks and scratches, each one annotated in fastidious script detailing the manner and date of its earning. His exposed face was likewise abused, those stretches of skin not torn up by battle wounds ritually scarred.

Koorland's own armour was battered, and he would not repaint it until his vengeance was won, but whereas his oath was exceptional, born out of grief, the practice of the Excoriators to preserve all hurts done to them was strange to him, as were the rituals of the others in the fleet: the Black Templars, the Crimson Fists, and the Fists Exemplar. Brotherhood brought them here to the gathering of the Last Wall – the successors of the old VII Legion amassed again as Terra was threatened. Despite their commonalities, fifteen hundred years had passed since the VII Legion had ceased to be, and these Chapters fathered by the same primarch had drifted far apart.

Was this how the Heresy began, Koorland wondered, brothers so distanced by circumstance that they ceased to recognise their own, and turned on one another? The man beside him shared his genetic gifts and a deep history. For all that, he was more a stranger than brother, someone to be greeted and feted at the Festival of Blades as an honoured guest, but one whose mind Koorland could never know. Surrounded by his warrior kin, the last of the Imperial Fists had never felt so alone, nor so exposed.

'So many of Dorn's sons gathered together in one place,' said Issachar. Beneath the fearsomeness that his damaged armour and scarification bestowed on him, Issachar was a considered man, and he spoke softly. 'The power concentrated here halts my breath. Such an army, such a fleet. With it, the stars are ours for the taking.' Issachar stepped closer to the armourglass of the window gallery and spread the fingers of one scratched gauntlet upon it, as if he would seize that power for himself. He smiled at Koorland, the knotted tissue on his face distorting the expression into something ugly.

'That is why the Legions are no more. And this is no Legion,' said Koorland, 'despite our numbers. At last count we are two thousand eight hundred of the line of Rogal Dorn. The Fists Exemplar are much depleted, High Marshal Bohemond calls in his crusades but they are scattered.' He left unsaid the fate of his own brothers, slaughtered at Ardamantua. 'Five companies of the Crimson Fists, eight of your brothers–'

'The rest will come,' reassured Issachar. 'We grow in strength daily. Soon the Excoriators will be here in full, every last battle-brother and neophyte. I swear this to you. The Iron Knights have responded to the call, and make their way to join us.'

'And then what? How many can we count upon? If all our brothers answer the call there will be fewer than four thousand of us.'

'High Marshal Bohemond keeps his own Chapter numbers a mystery – how many of them might come? And we have yet no word from the Soul Drinkers. They are secretive but honourable, and will have set out in force the moment they received the call to the Last Wall.'

'So five thousand, at best,' said Koorland. 'At the height of its power, the old Seventh consisted of over one hundred thousand warriors, and it was but one of eighteen Legions. How differently things would go were it still so.'

'The breaking was done long ago, brother. That was then and this is now. I have always honoured the decision, as the primarch eventually did. But lately I have come to see the other side.' Issachar gestured at the fleet. 'Look at us, divided by tradition, overwhelmed by enemies, betrayed by the men set to rule over us. Unable to bring sufficient strength to bear to truly crush our foes, we push them out only for them to slink back when our attention is drawn elsewhere.' He glanced uneasily at the triptych of tall bas-reliefs at the end of the gallery. The central depicted the Emperor surrounded by light, Black Templars at His feet, holding up their weapons. 'Some of us are fallen into superstition.'

'You do not know that,' said Koorland, yet he agreed in his hearts. To him the image looked like supplication.

'I look at our brothers' decorations, their temples and their honours. They hide it yet they flaunt it.'

Koorland examined the carvings. He shrugged away his own misgivings. 'Does it matter? Our Templar brothers are noble to a fault. A little headstrong, perhaps, but so was Sigismund of legend, and they say he was the favoured son of Dorn.'

'All my life I have fought with honour and determination,' said Issachar, 'to uphold the rule of the Emperor. Let others worship Him, those we shield know no better. To them the Emperor must seem as a god. But our gene-fathers walked by His side, they were His sons, created by His knowledge, not by sorcery. To think on the Emperor as a divinity is to confer the same upon His children, and by extension onto their offspring. We are far from divine. Yes, lord Chapter Master, it matters.'

'I am not Chapter Master, not truly. I cannot claim to have mastered myself, and I am all there is,' said Koorland.

Issachar searched Koorland's face a moment. 'The honour was thrust upon you, but I adjudge you worthy of the rank, brother. We are equals, you and I.'

'You do me a great honour by calling me brother. I shall attempt to command myself accordingly.'

'We do not listen to you lightly, brother. We require a leader. The Imperial Fists are the senior Chapter. Your assumption of command saves much dissension and loss of time.'

'I am a figurehead,' said Koorland.

'You are not.'

'Then it is a pity Bohemond only listens to me when he feels he must.'

'He has deferred leadership to you.'

'Then why do we not attack?' complained Koorland. 'Terra itself lies under the shadow of the Beast's moon and he plays for time, intent on attacking those nearest. His plan is strategically unsound.'

'He plays for numbers.'

Koorland's face creased with anguish. 'His pride threatens us all. He would not be so headstrong had he not been forced to fall back at Aspiria.'

'We are all hostage to our humours. You have lost much,' said Issachar. 'Do not let that colour your decisions.'

'I have lost everything, and we stand to lose the throneworld itself! How could we bear that, if the walls of the Palace should fail and no son of Dorn is there to man them?'

Issachar gripped the lip of Koorland's pauldron. 'It is not yet gone. The moon has not attacked. The orks are unaware of our gathering. Once there are a few more of us, then we shall drive at them. Calm yourself. You are a Chapter Master now. There are politics to consider.'

'Politics are what created this disaster.'

'Politicians created this disaster, brother. Politics are a part of life, unpalatable as it is.' Issachar slapped Koorland's shoulder. 'Come, why do we not test ourselves against one another? It is rare outside the Festival of Blades that our kind meet.'

'This is no time for empty tournaments.'

'That is not what I suggest. Let us hone our bladework,

brother, so that we might better slay the enemy. It is rarely we of Dorn's lineage cross blades, and there is a clarity that combat brings. It will help you, and be a great honour to me.'

'Honour?' said Koorland thoughtfully.

'We will spar?' said Issachar.

'Not now,' said Koorland. 'Later. I must speak with Bohemond first. You mention honour, I will appeal to his. This delay has gone on long enough.' Koorland strode out, brow furrowed.

'Shall I come with you?' called Issachar.

'No, brother,' Koorland shouted back. 'This confrontation needs to be face to face, and accomplished alone. I cannot rely on my allies to carry me through. The High Marshal must see me as strong.'

Issachar approved. Koorland was learning.

Bohemond received Koorland warmly in his sparely decorated quarters. Away from the splendidly ornate public sections of the *Abhorrence*, the few private areas Koorland had seen were spartan, almost monkish. Bohemond's rooms were no exception. Buried deep at the base of the ship's command spire, they were windowless, lacking adornment. Bohemond's plate was on a rack at the centre of a display of many weapons. A few trophies hung in stasis fields on the opposite wall. Weapons were the only indulgence the High Marshal permitted himself. A tall arch led through to his arming chambers, and through it could be glimpsed silent bondsmen going about their business attending to Bohemond's other armours and equipment.

The furniture was plain. Documents of pressing

importance were fastidiously arranged on the three tables. Koorland could not help but respect Bohemond more for this frugality.

His notion still hot in his mind, Koorland eschewed all formality and came straight to the point.

'We will depart tomorrow,' said Koorland.

'I advise against it,' said Bohemond. 'We are too few.' Bohemond's robes were plain too, a bone-coloured habit covered with a black surplice, the Templar's cross emblazoned in white upon the chest. Sigismund's sword, the badge of his office, was as ever belted at his side, a bolt pistol on his opposite hip. Everyone in Bohemond's Chapter, bondsman and brother alike, carried some sort of armament. The number of warrior bondsmen Koorland saw on the *Abhorrence* astounded him.

'We have insufficient numbers to ensure victory, it is true,' conceded Koorland, 'but there are enough of us to make it a possibility. What we lack is time. Terra is threatened, High Marshal. Your plan to target the nearest moon is laudable, but formulated before the throneworld was attacked. We must act.'

'Must we? What will you say when not only your Chapter is destroyed, Koorland, but most of four others? We must pick our battles carefully.'

'There is only one battle we must fight. We are the Last Wall. We will not fall. Our predecessors did not fall on Terra when all seemed lost. We will not fall now.'

Bohemond's face was a wreck, burned off by an ork psyker. Half was a metal mask, with a lidless augmetic eye. The rest was so scarred and lumpen he was almost devoid of human expression. 'Spoken like a true son of Dorn. I applaud your sentiment.' Bohemond poured himself a large measure of a spirit unfamiliar to Koorland. He proffered the bottle, Koorland shook his head, and Bohemond replaced it on the table.

'Allow me, if I may, to draw an analogy.'

'High Marshal, there is no time for stories–'

'It will take but a moment.'

'Very well,' said Koorland.

Bohemond gestured to a pair of plain metal chairs, and they sat down facing each other.

'Sigismund was a son of Dorn, and so highly favoured by the primarch that when my Chapter was founded under his auspices, he was granted one of Dorn's favourite vessels – the *Eternal Crusader* – to be the lynchpin of his efforts to extend the Imperium's reach. A great vessel, alas it languishes in refit in the shipyards of Cypra Mundi and will not be returned to us for twenty years. I feel its lack sorely.'

'Your point, High Marshal?'

Bohemond downed his drink. He gasped in satisfaction. His mouth no longer closed properly, and so a dribble spilled from his riven lips. He wiped them unselfconsciously on a cloth he drew from his sleeve. 'The *Eternal Crusader* represents the spirit of our Chapter and of our founder. Sigismund swore never to rest, that the Black Templars would not build walls but forge onward, performing the role the Emperor originally created us for – to unite the galaxy under the rule of man. Not to oversee its piecemeal dissolution under the guise of defence. The sons of Dorn are renowned as wall-keepers and castellans. Not so

the followers of Sigismund – for us attack is the only form of defence. Our blades are our parapets, our tanks are our fortresses, and never are they more effective than in the advance. Walls are of no use if the enemy is permitted to live outside the gate.'

Away from the council of Chapter Masters, Bohemond was risking more, goading the Imperial Fist directly. Koorland refused to rise to the bait. 'Then you think Terra is lost,' he said calmly.

As Koorland expected, Bohemond did not answer directly. Instead he said, 'Targets of greater opportunity present themselves to us, brother. We must strike now, and throw the orks into confusion. Should we kill three or four of their moons, they will be forced to deal with us. Strike at Terra, and we leave much of the Imperium to burn.'

'And so Terra will be lost. What then of the Emperor?'

A strange look crossed the remains of Bohemond's face. 'The Emperor is eternal.'

'At your waist, High Marshal, you carry the Sword of Sigismund.' Koorland pointed at Bohemond's great sword. 'Within it is bound a fragment of Dorn's own blade, broken in a rage when he failed to protect his lord. And yet you would willingly let the same happen again. Tell me, High Marshal, whose oaths are the more important to you? Those of your founder, who while a great warrior, the Emperor's Champion, the first Templar, was still but a Space Marine? Are those of your primarch not of a higher order, forged as he was by the Emperor Himself, and set above the common run of humanity for its betterment? Do you deny your father in favour of his son? Will you honour your oaths?'

Bohemond's gaze hardened. 'Do you accuse me of hypocrisy, Koorland?'

'I ask you to clarify your priorities, that is all. If there is an accusation of hypocrisy, it comes from within your own heart, and not from my lips.' Koorland leaned forward. 'We cannot always pursue the desires of our hearts, righteous as they might be.' He paused. 'You hold your *Eternal Crusader* as dearly as your oaths?'

'Absolutely. Both ship and oaths were the gift of Dorn.'

'But this, the *Abhorrence* that serves as your flagship while Sigismund's craft repairs, is it a good ship?'

Bohemond's eye narrowed. 'It is a fine ship, a righteous tool of the Imperium.'

'So you see, son of my father, the power of choice is not always ours to wield.' Koorland bladed his right hand and brought it down in a slow chop to point at Bohemond. 'At the gathering of the Last Wall at last watch today, I will command that we strike for Terra. And you will not demur, lord High Marshal, but heartily concur.'

Koorland turned on his heel and left before Bohemond could respond. Both hearts pounded hard in his chest, the secondary activated by stress levels he had felt at no other time outside conflict. Nevertheless, he permitted himself a smile.

The Black Templars would sail for Terra, or Bohemond was worth none of his regard at all.

TWO

The Palace of the God-Emperor

Far from the gates leading to eldar lands, the children of Isha bent their efforts to their race's salvation. The non-matter that made up the fabric of the tunnel was dim, sleeping. A minor branching to a nowhere world, none had trodden this path for many centuries, and it slumbered. The organic convolutions of the tunnel were barely wide enough to accommodate the party and their transport. It tapered away to nothing not far ahead, truncated by unnatural forces. A waysinger choir chanted interweaving melodies under the watchful gaze of Farseer Eldrad Ulthran, most ancient of his kind. Sorrow as thick as poison fog wreathed them all. To force an opening here spelled death to the eldar way-singers, and only a handful of their choir remained alive.

Shadowseer Lhaerial Rey waited with five more of Cegorach's own for egress. The song rose and fell, become more complicated with every passing hundredth. The way remained shut. Dressed in their motley, the Harlequins made a play of lounging and preening as their kin expended

their life force, a performance that celebrated through mockery the sacrifices of the others.

Though they seemed indolent, any who had seen the warrior dancers fight knew they could be up and moving, weapons in hands, in the blink of an eye. The other eldar – those on the path of mourning and service sent to bring the dying waysingers home, the warlock and the Dire Avengers sent to guard them – regarded the Harlequins with suspicion. Only the Dire Avengers showed no fear of them, but then they showed nothing at all.

The song of the waysingers faltered as another of their number collapsed, his soul fleeing into his waystone.

'Sing your song!' urged Eldrad Ulthran. He set his staff and bowed his ornate helm. The gems studding his wargear glowed with power as he poured more of his own might into the waysingers.

A gleaming slit ran down the side of the changeless stuff of the webway.

'Your song is one of power and beauty. Success is within our grasp! Your sacrifice will be remembered for a thousand cycles,' said Ulthran. 'A final effort, brothers and sisters – your deaths bind a favourable skein for the fate of Ulthwé! Sing, and usher in the rebirth of our race!'

With a melodic shout, the last of the waysingers fell dead, her dying breath sung out to open the path. Twenty of them had paid with their lives so that Lhaerial Rey could do what she must do, and their corpses littered the webway. Those sent to watch over them radiated sorrow. Lhaerial Rey did not grieve. One day Cegorach would free them all from death.

The webway parted to reveal a dark and soulless place beyond.

Ulthran approached the shadowseer. Lhaerial leapt to her feet, performing an elaborate bow.

'Take this token, given to me fifteen hundred cycles ago,' said Ulthran. He held out a large, finely carved tooth hanging from a chain. 'It will convince the *mon-keigh* of your deadly sincerity.' Lhaerial Rey took the tooth and spoke her gratitude with a gesture. Ulthran pointed his staff at the portal. 'Go! Go now! The door is open, but will not remain so for long.'

The webway spur convulsed in sudden peristalsis. The grav-barge that had borne the party there rocked, disturbed by shifts in the physics of that in-between realm. The attention of the Great Enemy pressed down upon the walls, whispering her seductive call to the annihilation of self that every eldar felt. The webway was damaged here, and perilous.

Lhaerial Rey's troupe tensed. No other but a Harlequin could see it, the micro-shifts in stance and muscle.

The doorway peeled itself back, just wide enough to admit a single eldar at a time.

'We dance,' said Lhaerial Rey.

In a bright flurry of shattering silhouettes, the Troupe of Joyful Tears departed the webway.

The hall on the far side of the portal was of lifeless stone, part-panelled in wood killed a thousand light years away and brought in slow-drying agony across the stars. This world was as dead as its ruler. The stink of humanity lay thick upon it, the statues near the ceiling coated in dust, the shed skin cells of people five hundred cycles gone. The psychic effect was a hideous weight, thousands of years of human suffering pressing in on Lhaerial's sensitive mind, and that was the least of it. Crushing the sensation of the dead of the Earth was the titanic presence of the Corpse Emperor.

Such power made Lhaerial's mind reel, and for a moment her contempt for the creatures of Terra wavered. The mind of the Emperor was a mountain in the surging madness of the Othersea, blinding in its brilliance. The Great Powers circled this place like razorshark waiting out the death throes of a void-whale. That terrible presence held them back, and all His little servants were ignorant of it! Unease gripped her, that she would be noticed by the Dark Gods or their defier, and the fragile flame of her being snuffed out.

The feeling passed. The regard of the things of the Othersea was ossified, so long had they fixed their gaze on the Earth. The Emperor did not shift His regard. His attention was elsewhere, upon the blinding pyre of souls, navigation beacon of the mon-keigh. She had no indication she was seen. There was little relief in that. She had laughed in the face of She Who Thirsts, but the Corpse Emperor filled her with a sense of dread.

Few among the eldar could stand to be in such a place. To the left and right, she saw her fellows go through the same stumble and recovery, their sensitive minds disturbed. When the dance resumed, their steps were heavier than before.

The troupe ran through the abandoned hall, their light tread leaving no trace in the dust. They were spears of light arrowing through the dark, outshining the dim lanterns set into the vaulting overhead. Carved saints, comical in their anguish and pomposity, loomed out of the dark. They came to a heavy iron door rusted as red as blood. Gehennelith somersaulted, power sword slashing down. His blow delivered, he leapt aside as the sisters Tueneniar and Linead concluded the portal's shattering with their shuriken pistols.

Lhaerial Rey was through first, her outline a shimmering cloud of diamonds. Gehennelith, Tueneniar, Linead, Barinamean came after, and lastly the death jester Bho, his *dathedi* spreading a cloud of ebon shards as confusing as a flurry of bats. Bho had his own reasons for coming, unknown to her. Whatever they were, she was glad of his presence.

A corridor stretched away, as dim and sepulchral as the hall they had left. A dead planet for a race that had doomed itself. Blue skies and seas, continent-spanning forests and millions of years of natural glory unsullied by crude humanity cried out to be remembered. It sickened her heart, she who had trod the nightmare ground of the Crone Worlds, who thought herself beyond such feeling. If Eldrad Ulthran himself had not requested her aid, she would never have set foot here.

Everywhere there was only silence, echoing avenues and empty rooms brimming with the self-importance of this race, so arrogant they had paved over the ground that fed them, uprooted the trees that nourished them and boiled away the seas that birthed them. Their crimes were lesser in scale than those of her own ancestors, perhaps, but their folly was worse for its crudeness. There was a majesty in the fall of the eldar, a glorious dance a million cycles in the making. Mankind was a moron chopping at the branch it stood upon. Black-hearted, close-minded, feeble-bodied. Humanity did not deserve to live. She danced out her hatred upon the flagstones as she ran.

Ulthran had chosen their insertion point well. The deaths of the waysingers bought them a stealthy entrance; these halls had been deserted for some time. The passing of their feet was as gentle as the pattering of rain on Terra's extinct forests. The few maintenance drones they saw, ghoulishly fashioned from the skulls of human dead, they shot down.

It could not last. They burst through a creaking set of doors into a hall that ran for several hundred lengths. High desks marched up both sides in precipitous tiers, hundreds of shelves rearing up over those. More dead wood lit by feeble lights of soulless electricity. The rough scent of humanity was strong there. The place was in disarray, sheets of paper and vellum and plasticised hydrocarbons scattered all about.

They saw their first humans. Pallid things, lumpenly ugly even by the woefully low standards of the race. Several dozen cowered together beneath the desk tiers. Their dull, animal eyes were fixed on the dirty plex-glass of the ceiling a hundred lengths overhead. They did not see the Harlequins until they were practically past them, a kaleidoscopic zephyr that stirred their scattered papers.

Whole family groupings hid together. They had never seen the sun, Lhaerial could sense it. One of their young let out a mewling cry. Lhaerial's domino-masked face whipped round, looking the human child full in the face. She raised her pistol, but her mind balked at activating it. The girl's expression was suffused with a terrified wonder. Her eyes glistened at the beauty she saw. Lhaerial vaulted over a fallen lectern, and put her pistol up.

The Harlequins were already gone by the time the scribes began shouting. An alarm bell tolled out shortly after.

Rune signifiers shone on the map projected into Lhaerial's mind by her wargear. They were closing on their destination, at the very edge of the administrative hives. Six thousand lengths or more to their target.

They emerged at speed into a metal cavern. Under steel skies a vast, decrepit parkland opened up, dotted with huge mansions, the fiefs of petitioner-barons and pensioned scrivener overseers. Light pipes directed weak sunlight into the park. Once it had been a lush place, but many of the trees were dead, skeletal things stark white in the gloom. Scraggly weeds dominated the few patches of day.

Through dirty-mouthed tunnels, ill-disciplined groups of soldiers in black streamed to oppose the Harlequins.

Gehennelith flipped effortlessly over streaking las-bolts, felling several of the humans with shots of pinpoint accuracy: one disc, one kill.

'Dance their deaths and let us be on,' ordered Lhaerial. 'They are weak, but they are many, and we have stirred their ire.'

Truly she spoke, for already Tueneniar had become separated from her troupe mates. Bho's shuriken cannon wailed as it spat out its deadly gifts. Men ran in terror as the shrieker cannon's mutagens caused their fellows to explode.

+Make your own way, little dancer. Distract them so that

I may complete our task. We shall meet again,+ communicated Lhaerial. +In Cegorach's circle, if not in the flesh.+

Tueneniar sent her assent. She vaulted over the heads of her foes and onto the lowest balcony of a hanging garden that stretched most of the way to the glassed-out sky. In moments she was gone.

'Shadowseer!' said Linead. 'We must all diverge, draw them away, perform alone for our audience and draw their attention away from you.'

'Agreed.' Lhaerial landed softly in the midst of a group of men. Five artful strokes of her sword slew them all. They fell away together, dead before they hit the torn grass. Las-fire converged on her position, but she was already away, running tirelessly towards her target. 'Break the circle, travel your solitary skeins, my faithful. I shall see you before the Golden Throne of the mon-keigh Emperor, if that is what Morai-Heg has woven.'

Klaxons clamoured. Linead tossed a grenade through an ornate window. An explosion shook the mansion, spreading fire into its gardens. Lucifer Blacks poured into the area.

Lhaerial sprinted for the end of the park. A large block of men had taken up station there. They were forming lines, hoping to bring her down with massed volleys. A few took opportunistic shots as they organised themselves, but she effortlessly curved around them. Leaping and somersaulting, she soared high over the first ranks before they could give ordered fire. Hallucinogen grenades popped out of the fluted launcher on her back, bursting into gas clouds of scintillating colours among the humans. Their weak minds were instantly affected. She bent the hallucinations they experienced into illusions of awful nightmare, and they ran weeping before her.

Then she was away, and her fellows too, scattering like leaves in the wind, leaving the Lucifer Blacks flailing and disorganised. They trod solitary paths, save Bho, who followed her. As always he never spoke his mind, simply acted. Once again, she was glad of his presence.

Seven hundredths of a cycle later, an explosion rolled out down the endless tunnels and ways of the Imperial Palace, their planned diversion. She smiled behind the mirror bowl of her mask. Everything was going to plan.

THREE

Krule's dance

The Great Chamber of the Senatorum Imperialis was in pandemonium at the explosions in the Palace, moments after the departure of the ork ambassador. Fearing a new offensive against them, the nerve of the great and good of the Imperium broke. Prefectii and consularies wrestled with menials and aides as the exits clogged with human bodies. They scrambled over each other, trampling their fellows in their rush to escape.

Drakan Vangorich, Grand Master of the Officio Assassinorum, grabbed Mercado and shook him.

'Where are the eldar?' demanded Vangorich.

Mercado looked at him dumbly. 'The Viridarium Nobiles, five levels down.'

'That's only five kilometres from the Sanctum Imperialis.'

Mercado nodded. His eyes were still wide, his fingers limp around his vox-horn. Vangorich came close to killing the captain of the Lucifer Blacks there and then.

'How many?'

'Reports are confused–'

'How *many?*' spat Vangorich through gritted teeth.

'A handful, seven or eight. Brightly coloured.' The man was rallying himself. 'I'll direct all my men to the defence of the Throne Room, and inform Captain-General Beyreuth.'

'I'm sure he's well aware of this breach,' said Vangorich. 'Send your men, but they'll be too late.'

'Where are you going?' called Mercado as Vangorich shoved his way through the crowd.

'To deal with this myself.' He lifted his sleeve to his mouth and spoke into the vox-bead hidden in a button there. 'Krule, I need you. Now.' He changed channels. 'Veritus, if you can hear me, meet me at the Sanctum.' No reply was forthcoming.

Vangorich headed for the ablutorials. Near the exits from the main chamber the press of the crowd was slackening as the cream of the Terran adepta flailed at each other in their panic to escape. At the centre the crush grew as men and women shoved their way down from the stacked ranks of seats. The Twelve had already gone from the High Table, whisked away by their bodyguards. At least, thought Vangorich, the Lucifer Blacks can do something correctly.

He wove his way through the crowd with smooth and occasionally violent efficiency, his habitual insouciant amble cast away in favour of a predator's fluid movement. Many recognised him and did their best to get out of his way. Where they did not, he helped them along with fists and sharp elbows. By a wash fountain he depressed an insignificant cherub's elbow. A hidden door slid open. Vangorich slipped into the tunnel it revealed. He hurried along its dark length, emerging into dim sunlight high on the south wall of the Great Chamber of the Senatorum Imperialis.

He hurried groundwards through a network of concealed maintenance ladders and catwalks. Overhead the ork moon hung pale in the washed-out sky. He glanced at it periodically. No activity there, for the moment. Perhaps the ork ambassador had not yet returned. What the result of his embassy would be was anyone's guess. Events were getting ahead of Vangorich.

Still, he thought. One thing at a time.

At the bottom, Krule awaited him in the groundcar of a rich man. The blood of the prior owner was still wet on the dashboard.

'We need to get to the Sanctum,' he said.

'The roads are blocked,' said Krule, getting out of the car. 'I know a way. We need to take the high-lines.' He pointed to a transport hub some hundred yards away. Pods rolled automatically into the station from their wire tracks as calmly as if this were any other day.

They ran through the crowds spilling from the Grand Chamber into the plaza, and down onto the Daylight Way. The transit terminus sat in the shadow of the high wall. People bunched around the terminus, fighting to get onto its boarding platforms. Krule battered his way through, Vangorich behind him. They hurled the people clambering into a waiting pod aside. The crowd recoiled, then surged back towards the open door, until Krule caved in the face of the lead man with a deadly punch. The crowd shrank back again, and Krule slammed the door shut.

Vangorich activated the pod with his signum, and it rose rapidly on creaking cables, leaving the boiling crowds below.

Through yellowed plastek windows, they looked down on the Senatorum sector of the Imperial Palace. The highways were choked with the private vehicles of dignitaries and the nobility. Lesser streets were filled with civilians on their knees, wailing out panicked prayers and blocking the way for those trying to escape. Fights erupted, threatening riot. With nowhere to go, people simply ran back and forth madly, driven by adrenaline to do something, anything, in the face of the inevitable. The sky was crowded with aircraft and flocks of servo-constructs as thick as the crowds on the ground. The ork moon loomed high overhead, intent unknown, its brutal face frozen in mirth at the uproar it had caused.

'Emperor help us if this is the best we can muster to save ourselves,' said Vangorich. He was no believer in the faith, but it truly would take a god to solve this mess.

Beast Krule remained mute. It was weirdly calm in the pod, the violence beneath played out in silence. The wire the pod depended on headed up and down the multi-layered hives seemingly at random. Vangorich overrode the system, preventing the pod from halting. At transit stops horrified faces whipped by. The pod plunged on, drawn on by the vast, mountain-sized edifice of the Sanctum Imperialis. The heart of the Imperium grew, dominating everything, a prison and a lens for the might of the being trapped within. The pod shifted lines, following a high track that led up and up. The wrinkled skin of the city dropped rapidly away.

Krule stood. 'Vent spire,' he said, pointing to a

cathedral-tower chimney that pointed vaingloriously at the attack moon.

The Assassins stopped the pod as it passed over a balcony jutting from the spire. They smashed the door and dropped down, broke their way into a maintenance portal, pushed their way past the herd of servitors who lived within the tower, and descended down into the upper levels of the endless inner hives of the Imperial Palace.

They descended many levels, flying down stairs, ignoring elevators and lift platforms, heading always for the chatter of military vox and reports of the intruders. Eventually, they found their prey.

Vangorich emerged into a machine hall thundering with the business of renewing the throneworld's atmosphere, deep below the false metal surface of Terra. Stale air hooted down plasteel tubes, drawn by pistons driven by giant flywheels, to be bubbled through lake-deep tanks of ancient glass clotted with algae. On the gantries over them a sole, gaudy alien battled single-handedly against a company of Astra Militarum.

'There!' said Vangorich.

A hundred men were set against the eldar. They crept towards it along the grid of catwalks. Following any law of engagement, it should have been overwhelmed many times over. Corpses littered the mesh over the water, their blood staining the algae black. All of them were human.

'We must question it,' said Vangorich.

'It will die before we can get to it,' said Krule.

The eldar executed a flawless leap. Its form broke into a confusing trail of glimmering diamonds that twisted twenty

metres over the soupy mess of the tanks. Its weapon hissed, and a stream of discs cut down three men before its feet touched steel again. The human commander shouted, directing his men to block the alien's escape routes. Las-beams cut through the air, but the alien danced over them.

'I doubt that,' said Vangorich. 'Those men are outmatched.'

'Then I'll see to it,' said Krule.

The eldar pranced into a squad of Lucifer Blacks, slaying seven with its sword. Not one of them came close to landing a return blow. Vangorich grabbed Krule's shoulder. 'Beast, this is one of their warrior dancers. I thought them a legend, but evidently they are not.'

'And?' said Krule.

'And be careful.'

Krule looked at him incredulously. 'You've never warned me before.'

'There is, as they say, a first time for everything. This is one of those times.' Vangorich released his Assassin. Krule snorted dismissively.

Krule came at the eldar when it was only metres from a wide service vehicle exit. Three dirty yellow power loaders had been drawn across the exit to prevent the eldar's escape, the gaps between jammed haphazardly with crates of algal feedstock. Soldiers fired wildly over their barricade, desperate to bring the killer down before it got among them. The eldar leapt out of the way of every shot with stunning agility, every flip and twist bringing it nearer. A final leap, a sword of bright silver glinting in the dim light. Shurikens whickered through the air. In moments the Guardsmen were dead.

Their deaths, though quick, gave Krule the time he needed to draw near.

'Stop!' he called.

The eldar halted, poised on the cab roof of a wheeled loader. It cocked its head at Krule. A white domino mask covered its face, one black tear sliding down the cheek over and over again. Close-fitting motley clad its body. For all the eldar's otherworldly slenderness its limbs rippled with muscle.

Krule advanced. The eldar leaped backwards over his head, its body shattering into a blizzard of geometric shapes. The alien somersaulted through four complete turns as it flew, its true form barely visible as a fuzzy outline in a field of spinning diamonds. Krule's chronaxic implants kicked in, chemical stimulants overloading his metabolism and sending his heartbeat into a continuous blur. His sense of time slowed to the point he could have slipped between the raindrops of a storm. The alien was still faster.

A hail of discs shot out of the alien's pistol, the feed-mag disappearing upwards. Krule dodged three; a fourth sliced into his bicep, embedding itself in the adamantium reinforcing his humerus. He suppressed the pain, wheeling over in a scissoring cartwheel, driving his feet at the alien. The eldar leaned back so far his crest of hair brushed the bloodied floor. Krule sprang off his hands onto his feet, and aimed a devastating punch, but the xenos wove out of the way, spinning around and bringing its pistol to bear again. Krule slapped the gun off target just as a spray of deadly discs hissed from its snout. He evaded the humming power sword that followed. The eldar flipped backward over and over, firing as it went. Krule dived aside, a storm of shurikens following him. His eyes flicked to the creature's broad girdle. Some kind of grav-belt.

The eldar spread its arms and flipped towards him, bouncing lightly from the catwalk guardrail. Krule charged at it, dropping to his side and sliding under a further fusillade of discs. He scooped up a lasrifle still sticky with blood, and fired. The eldar leaned casually out of the shot's way and bisected the lasgun with its sword. The metal and plastek came apart with a bang. Krule fended off further strikes with the smoking butt of the gun. He swung at the flat of the eldar's blade, more of his improvised weapon disintegrating with every parry.

The eldar cartwheeled at him, flicked its sword down into the ground and used it as a pivot to swing around the hilt, feet out, catching Krule full in the face. The Assassin staggered back, and the eldar moved in for the kill, but Krule was feigning concussion. As the eldar drove its sword at Krule he stepped sideways, shifting his stance so that he came outside the eldar's arm. He grabbed the alien's girdle, and tore it free. The eldar danced back, but not fast enough. Krule grabbed its sword wrist and slammed the heel of his palm into its elbow, shattering the delicate bone. It took the blow without a sound. The sword fell from its limp hand to dangle by its power feed. The alien rolled along Krule's arm, until the two were as tightly pressed as dance partners.

'You fight well for a human,' it said in accented Gothic. The smooth golden snout of its weapon pressed under his chin.

A *crack* shattered the moment. The eldar fell, a smoking hole in its temple beside its mask.

Vangorich stood behind, his hand out, the ring of his digital laser exposed over his knuckle. He sucked at his flesh
where the discharge had singed his skin and shook out his
fingers with a pained expression.

'I told you to be careful.'

Krule looked at his fallen foe. It seemed so fragile dead, its
limbs thin as reeds, more like the doll of a rich upper-hive
child than a creature that had lived and breathed. His hand
went to the disc embedded in his bicep. He cut his fingers
on it as he tried to pull it out, for it was lodged fast in the
metal and bone of his upper arm.

Vangorich strode over to the dead alien. 'These are their
elite of elite. We were lucky to kill it.'

Krule left the disc where it was. He flexed his fist. 'It hurts
like hell.'

'Do you know, Krule, one of the reasons I have always
enjoyed your company is that you never say anything asi-
nine like "I had it covered" or other such nonsense.'

'I didn't. I'd be dead without you.' Krule spoke quietly. He
was panting hard, and sweat and blood ran from his skin.
He had never come this close to being beaten.

'Quite. The question is, what is it doing here? I wanted to
interrogate it. It's a shame I had to kill it to save you, but
I had no choice. I could not cripple it. Their weapons are
mentally operated, so it was the head or it was nothing.'

'You have my thanks.'

'Save them. In not too long a time the ork ambassador
will be back aboard the attack moon, and you may yet die
today.' Vangorich stroked at his scar in thought. 'Only seven
or so, Mercado said. That's an awfully small number to try

anything meaningful at the Palace, even for xenos as arrogant as the eldar. I am not so sure all is as it seems here.
Come, we had better go, or there will be none of the xenos
left to question.'

FOUR

Before the Throne

Lhaerial came to the outer precincts of the Sanctum Imperialis. Bho the death jester followed her, close as a shadow. For as long as they could they avoided combat, she clouding the weak minds of the humans where possible, detouring to avoid them where it was not. They followed half-forgotten conduits and filthy service ducts, coming ever closer to their target. The blazing light of the Emperor's beacon grew in her mind's eye, blotting out her limited ability to read the skein. Her future was a mystery to her now, and she must act cautiously.

One by one she felt the death songs of her fellows, fallen in solo dances with no audience to applaud. A black wave of despair rose in her heart, but she froze it. Sorrow could wait for a time when it could be turned into laughter, a celebration of her troupers' joining with Cegorach.

There came a moment when they could hide no more, at the place where the architecture of the Palace opened up and became dominated by the vast avenues radiating from the Throne Room. The weak infantry in black were replaced by armoured giants, their golden plate draped in sombre black cloaks. Their species aside, there was nothing similar between the two breeds of warrior. These were the Adeptus Custodes, and few could stand against them.

Lhaerial had expected to encounter them sooner, for Ulthran had told her they guarded all parts of the Palace in the days when the Emperor lived. Time had made them cautious, and they gathered now only around the Throne Room of their lord, careful of what little mortal life remained to Him.

The secret tunnels turned away from the Throne Room, and Bho and Lhaerial were forced out. They avoided the main processional way and its progression of mighty, symbolic gates, taking a lesser avenue – still many hundred lengths across, the vaulting of the ceiling lost to smoke and distance. Only one gateway barred this avenue, at the entrance to the antechamber. Far away down the mighty road it hid in clouds of incense.

'This way, Bho, come!'

The Adeptus Custodes waited for them, opening fire as they ran down the vast processional way. Hard projectiles of metal whined past them, shot from the tips of long-hafted weapons as heavy as Lhaerial herself. Primitive, as all the technology of the humans was, but deadly. Just one round, were it to hit, would obliterate her slender body.

They did not hit.

Lhaerial wove around the bolts. Bho fired from behind, his screamer cannon punching the genetically enhanced warriors from their feet. They were too mighty to be felled by the shot itself, instead dying painfully as the gene-toxins in the shrieker rounds rewrote their life code explosively.

'Stop, stop!' she called out in their ugly language. 'My name is Lhaerial Rey,' she continued, 'Shadowseer of the Ceaseless Song. I come here at command of Eldrad Ulthran to deliver a message of great import to the Emperor of Mankind!'

Only murder dwelled in their hearts. A giant moved to intercept her, his great halberd whirling in buzzing arcs around his head. This one moved with a grace and speed she did not associate with the humans. She fought ferociously with him, trading parries and ripostes like for like, the sheer strength of the human shocking her. She saluted him before she took his head from his shoulders. 'Friendship! Friendship!' she cried out, Gothic's coarseness an affront to her tongue.

More of them came at her, shouting angrily. That she was swinging her sword at them probably belied her words, she thought ironically, but she refused to die for their idiocy. She called out as she killed, over and over again. 'My name is Lhaerial Rey, Shadowseer of the Ceaseless Song. I come here at command of Eldrad Ulthran to deliver a message of great import to the Emperor of Mankind. Friendship! Friendship! Cease your fighting!'

Bho shot down the last of them. Lhaerial vaulted the human's writhing form.

'The gate!' she cried to Bho. 'It is near!' Incredibly, the gate remained open, a sign of the humans' arrogance. A stream of Adeptus Custodes flooded forth.

The Harlequins sprinted on, launching themselves over the heads of those who came to oppose them; cutting down any who came within striking distance and ignoring the rest, Lhaerial expected a lucky shot to take her in the back at any moment.

'My name is Lhaerial Rey, Shadowseer of the Ceaseless Song. I come here at command of Eldrad Ulthran to deliver a message of great import to the Emperor of Mankind. Friendship! Friendship!'

The warriors of the Emperor would not listen, and the nearer they came to the Throne Room, the more furious they became. She only hoped that if she could get to the centre of the warding circles that girdled the Palace for thousands of lengths, her mind could touch His.

The door came closer, monumentally huge. She had rarely seen its like in the realm of flesh and matter. Only in the webway were such things to be seen, and they were the works of long ago. It towered five hundred lengths high, covered in ornate carvings too small to be made out, and fashioned from precious materials harvested from the entire galaxy. Doubtless this adornment concealed armoured plating many lengths deep.

The doors began to close. She and Bho ran faster, veering towards the bastion guarding the left of the doors. As they neared she put away her pistol and flicked a small ovoid of warm wraithbone from a pouch at her belt. The gates were closing with the steady certainty of glaciers grinding down mountains. A line of Custodians barred the way in front of the gates, halberds levelled and firing. Bho slew three with wailing shots of his cannon. His skill was marvellous to see.

He leapt and dived, somersaulting over its barrel. He fired all the while, unencumbered by the shrieker's great length.

Lhaerial arced over a wall of crested helms, and tossed the device into a vision slit in the bastion. There was a mellow flash as it discharged, spraying the room with a burst of softly glowing microscopic constructs. They pattered onto the walls, burrowing into the fabric of the building and attacking its systems. Eldar technology millions of years old overwhelmed the simple machines of the humans without difficulty. Their motive mechanisms suborned by the superior craft of her race, the gates ceased their closing barely a length apart. She and Bho jumped, threading the gap as a blaze of shells exploded all round the door edges.

On the other side was a hall bigger than all but the widest craftworld domes. On the far side were the great gates to the Sanctum Imperialis, wherein languished the morbid Emperor of Mankind. Twin Titans guarded it, poorly fashioned to resemble hounds, and festooned with vulgar attempts at art. They started towards her clumsily, jogging across the court and opening fire. Bursts of shattered metal and rock jumped skyward. She somersaulted between the impacts as the Warhounds tracked her. The noise of their discharge obliterated all senses, and Lhaerial danced through the thunder. The war machines ceased firing as she sought shelter among the ranks of the enemy.

They were so close to their goal. Lhaerial could feel the lessening of the Palace's psychic defences. They were nearing the centre of the wards. She called out with her mind to the Lord of Man. There came no reply, but lines of Adeptus Custodes running at them. The great gates were far away.

For a moment her heart faltered. She could not succeed. But she must try.

Bho was surrounded, attacking his foe with the great energy scythe affixed to the end of his gun. He slew four of theirs before he fell, shot from so many angles even his reflexes could not save him. As in life, he died silently. Lhaerial fought on, slaughtering her way through the humans as their war machines neared and slowed, stalking the edge of the melee. Were she to kill every one of the Adeptus Custodes, she would be obliterated immediately. Her progress slowed, the foe became too many; they were too accomplished as warriors. Their finest individuals would be a close match for her skills, and there were hundreds of them. She despaired. Her arms dropped.

'Peace! Peace!' she called.

She was brought down, wrestled to the floor by a dozen heavy arms.

Their leader forced his way towards her, his movements awkward with rage. He wore identical gold armour to all the others, but for a tall distinguishing plume of purple. Now would be the time to present the token, he was the one, but her arms were pinned and she could not move.

'My name is Lhaerial Rey, Shadowseer of the Ceaseless Song. I come here at command of Eldrad Ulthran to deliver a message of great import–'

The blow was almost too quick for her to see. It struck her mirror mask hard, snapping her head painfully to the side.

'Silence!' roared the leader. 'You come here shouting friendship as you slaughter your way towards the Lord of Mankind.'

A circle of boltguns pointed at her head.

'And now you will die.'

'Hold!' cried Vangorich. He and Krule rushed into the ante-chamber of the Sanctum Imperialis, a space big enough to station an army in. Though there was no army, war had recently visited. To the right, halfway to the Ultimate Gate, beyond which sat the Emperor Himself, a dozen Adeptus Custodes lay dead on the ground, a single, skull-masked eldar among them. The mosaic floor was cracked and ruined. Craters in the walls guttered with burning metal, damage from Titan weapons fire. A circle of Adeptus Custodes surrounded something hidden in its centre. 'Hold!'

Four warriors stepped into Vangorich's path, their guardian spears crossed. Their massive armoured bodies formed a wall he could not see over.

'Let me through! It is I, High Lord Vangorich.'

'Grand Master Vangorich?' shouted a commanding voice. The warriors parted, revealing their leader.

'Captain-General Beyreuth! I must beg your indulgence. Do not execute the prisoner! We must interrogate it.' Vangorich pushed his way into a forest of metal giants. Beyreuth waved them aside and he came to their captive: a female, by the shape of her. She was kneeling, beaten. Her clothes were brightly coloured and patterned, though dirtied with battle's smirch. Her face was hidden by a featureless mask of silver, and this was flawless. A thicket of blades pointed at her, the bolters mounted on the backs of the spearheads ready to obliterate her at a word.

'She has already tried to trick us with talk of parley,' said

Beyreuth. 'I will not consider her release so close to the Golden Throne. Most of this breed are witches, who knows what she plans? She has breached the Emperor's innermost sanctuary. For this insult she must and will pay.'

'Parley? What did she say?' said Vangorich.

The eldar spoke for herself, her voice thick with blood. 'My name is Lhaerial Rey, Shadowseer of the Ceaseless Song. I come here at command of Eldrad Ulthran to deliver a message of great import to the Emperor of Mankind.'

'Lies,' spat Beyreuth.

'Captain-general, please!' said Vangorich.

'You, the lord of killers, and you make a plea for her life?' said Beyreuth. 'Or is it only humans your kind kills?'

'I understand you are angry, furious, but we must be cautious,' said Vangorich. 'Orks are in the sky, and these xenos come alone. What if she is telling the truth?'

'I am being cautious. It is a lack of caution that led to the arrival of the orks. We cannot afford any further mistakes.' He raised his hand.

'I order you to stop!' shouted Vangorich.

'You are a High Lord, and a member of the Senatorum Imperialis, but your office is no longer numbered among the High Twelve. You have no authority to command me. None have, save the Emperor Himself.'

'Then this will prove sufficient!' called Inquisitor Veritus. The boots of his power armour rang on the mosaic floor as he stamped into the chamber, his Inquisitorial seal held high. Storm troopers fanned out either side of him, training their guns on the Adeptus Custodes.

'I am Veritus, and I am of the High Twelve. By this sigil I

wield the authority of the Emperor. While He cannot speak, the Inquisition are His voice.'

Beyreuth uttered something that might have been a sigh or a curse. He gestured, and his warriors stood back.

'I am so glad you could make this latest emergency, Veritus,' said Vangorich. 'After you departed the Senatorum so dramatically, I feared we had lost your good offices permanently.'

'Don't be facetious, Vangorich.'

Vangorich twitched his eyebrows. 'If I am facetious, it is merely because I find myself in a world governed by idiocy. I laugh, or I despair. You have arrived in the nick of time.'

'I got your message. I had to gather my forces. I am here now.'

'A reply would have been polite,' said Vangorich.

The three men looked down upon the captured eldar. Vangorich's spine shuddered as her faceless bowl mask looked back. A quiet power surrounded her.

'Why should we believe your protestations of friendship?' demanded Veritus.

'I have upon my person a token,' said the eldar, 'given by the Primarch Vulkan to the Farseer Eldrad Ulthran during your recent civil war.'

Veritus looked to the Custodians.

'You may take it out. If it is a trick, you shall die,' said Beyreuth.

Lhaerial reached into a small pouch strapped to her thigh. From it she removed an object and passed it to Veritus. The inquisitor's power armour whined as he reached for it.

He opened his hand. In it was a large tooth, capped with exquisitely worked gold.

'A tooth of a Nocturnian salamander. It could be as you say. These creatures are found only on Vulkan's home world. But how do I know this is not a trick, and that it was Vulkan who gave this to your master?'

'I have no master save the Laughing God,' said Lhaerial. 'That token is all I have to prove my good intent. If you do not value it, then Eldrad Ulthran underestimated you. My task is done and my life is forfeit. I die laughing at the fools that would not listen to sense.'

Veritus growled deep in his throat. 'The orks are at our door and an alien witch wishes to speak with the Emperor,' he said. He folded his fist over the tooth. 'We must take her away from here. It is not safe to have her kind so close to the Emperor.'

'You are to take her to the Inquisitorial Fortress?' asked Vangorich.

Veritus nodded. 'Wienand is there. I shall deal with two problems in one.'

'Then I suggest you hurry,' said Vangorich. 'The orks will move soon.'

Lhaerial spoke. 'You have far less time than you realise.'

FIVE

Woman in the moon

There were mountains that walked, and people trapped beneath them. A looped segment of time that Galatea Haas could not escape played repetitively in her dreams. The Proletarian Crusade was trapped between two walls of grinding metal and stone, coming together with awful finality. A wave of blood bore down on her, carrying terrified screams that suddenly cut out.

Haas came awake with a jolt, hands scraped raw through gripping the rough stone of her resting place. She was hidden at the back of a narrow cranny, high up the wall of a tunnel more crevasse than corridor. Her ears strained to pick out whatever it was that had disturbed her from the constant noise of the attack moon. Clanking mechanisms pounded ceaselessly, unshielded and raucous. After the disaster she had passed through one of the orks' machine halls, and her ears rang for hours afterwards. From the racket, it must have been only one of many hundreds of similar rooms.

Her flight from the doors was a jumble, a terrible memory broken into meaningless flashes of incident. Somehow, she had escaped. Drenched in the blood of the Crusaders, she had run through rough-hewn corridors and gaping natural caves. She was sure of discovery. Only her training and her will had kept her from succumbing to fear. But no one had found her, and eventually, exhausted, she had found this place, and fallen into a troubled sleep.

Something was close. She heard piping voices, far too high to be orks. Cautiously she put her head out over the lip of rock.

Three of the little creatures that served the orks were passing below, carrying small metal boxes and shoving at each other in malicious high spirits. The sight of them made her skin crawl. There was something worse about these beings than their masters. They were humpbacked and crooked. They rolled along with a sly gait. She imagined them stealing into homes in the dead of night, seeking out young to devour. Creatures from story, they seemed. Until yesterday she had had no idea they existed.

They were filthy, and they stank worse than the dirtiest man. How they smelled her over their own noisome reek was a surprise, but they did.

The leader stopped directly under her hiding place, its followers running into its back. They tittered horribly, provoking the leader to slap them into silence. It held up a finger for quiet. Nose twitching, it turned its head upward. Haas snatched her head back just in time.

The leader jabbered at one of the others. The second's ears drooped and the third laughed at its comrade. An argument ensued, finishing in more blows. Quiet fell. A moment later, a dirty green head appeared over the edge of Haas' hiding place. Its ears shot up in surprise as it saw Haas staring back at it.

The creature squealed as she swatted it with her shock maul. The weapon was designed for the suppression of civil disorder, but cranked up to full output it could deliver a fatal blow, and the slave orks were small. The creature flew against the wall, shrieking horribly. It impacted with a wet splat, and slid to the uneven floor, smoke pouring out of its ears. She levered herself out of the gap and fell between the other two.

They were poor fighters, but aggressive. They attacked together, raking at her with filthy fingernails, ripping the regimental uniform issued to her for the Crusade to tatters and scoring the skin underneath with burning scratches. She was fortunate that her enforcer's armour protected her from the worst of it.

The leader went down, its pointed head sporting a new and fatal dent. The last gibbered and shrilled in the orkish tongue, flailing at her with arms that were too long for its body. Its pointed nose and ears flapped as it jumped onto her, trying to throttle her with grasping, greasy fingers. She gasped for air. Pointed yellow teeth snapped millimetres from her nose, spattering her with saliva. She fell backward to the ground, luck more than effort putting her maul in the right place. She slammed the butt into its eye. It screamed and reared up. She scrambled backward and caved its ribs in with a panicked swipe.

Panting hard, she pushed the dead creature from her legs.

The energy of fear left her, and she struggled to get herself upright. Her head swam. She had not eaten since the Crusade had departed, and was so hungry she considered going through the slaves' filthy clothes to find some morsel of food or drink, but was not yet so desperate that she could bring herself to do it.

Numbly, she stared at the corpses.

A noise made her start.

By a kink in the corridor, framed in dull ruddy light, a fourth creature stood staring at her with wide red eyes, ears flat against its head in fear.

'Throne!' she exclaimed.

The creature's thin-lipped mouth worked wordlessly. Suddenly, it dropped its burden, turned on its heels and fled, squealing out a shrill alarm.

'No, no, no, no, no!' she shouted, staggering after.

The creature was fast, moving with a bounding scamper that she struggled to match. It cast terrified looks behind it at her, shouting without pause as it ran. Her throat burned with thirst and the polluted air of the moon, and the creature was gaining ever more ground.

Haas raced round a corner to see it diving through a crack between two armoured plates bolted to the rock. Haas threw herself after. Anything could be on the other side, but if the creature raised the alarm, she was dead anyway.

With relief, she saw it was all alone, quaking against a wall ahead, arms spread wide on the stone.

Hefting her maul, she approached.

A giant hand cuffed her across the back of the head, sending her sprawling face first into the rock. Stars swam in front of her eyes. She got to her hands and knees, blood flowing from her mouth. Something slammed into her neck. Wide metal jaws closed around her throat with a click. She grabbed at them futilely as she was hoisted high. Almost gently, the pole shifted around, bringing her face to face with the ork holding it.

Her captor regarded her with curious eyes glinting from eye sockets like caves. Its jaw was covered in a beard of bright but dirty hair, and more of the same crested its head. A single ivory fang, as long as Haas' forearm, jutted from the left side of its mouth. The damn thing was smiling at her, its eyes twinkling with vicious humour.

It rumbled something in the tongue of the orks. Haas raised her maul. It shook its head and flicked a switch on the haft of its catchpole. A massive shock cracked out from the jaws, and Haas fell unconscious.

'She's coming round,' said a man's voice.

'Be quiet, Marast, you'll have One Tooth in here on us!' hissed another.

'Looks different,' said the one called Marast. 'She's not one of us. She's a standard.'

'So? The galaxy's crawling with them. Give her something to drink, for the Emperor's sake.'

'It means, Huringer, that we're somewhere else, do you see? We've moved away from home,' said the first irritably.

'Don't talk to me like I'm stupid!' said Huringer.

'Don't be stupid, then. This armour too, enforcer or arbitrator, I'd say. But those badges aren't like anything I've ever seen.'

A canteen was pressed to Haas' lips. Warm, metallic water spilled into her mouth. She coughed, and swallowed gratefully. Her head felt heavy as a boulder, but she struggled up onto her elbows anyway.

There was not much light but it hurt her eyes. She was in a sweltering cell plated with metal. There was one door, a small grille at the top of it letting in a little light from outside. A little more came from a buzzing lumen globe dangling from a bare wire in the middle of the room.

Two odd-looking faces peered at her. She squinted until they came into focus, and pushed herself back in alarm when they did. Bald heads with pronounced eyes looked back, their owners crouching on unnaturally long legs.

'What are you?' she said. Her stomach rolled with nausea.

'Oh, that's charming. Very nice,' said the one called Marast. 'People, that's what we are. If you don't like us, we can call the orks. Maybe they'll give you a waking you'd prefer?'

Haas blinked. They were human, of a sort, but stretched in the body. Her eyes strayed to their legs.

'Guess she's never seen a longshanks before,' muttered Huringer.

Marast patted his leg with a thin-fingered hand. 'That's what we are. Don't stare so – in here you're the odd one out.'

'You're... mutants?'

'Abhumans!' said Huringer angrily. 'We're loyal subjects of the Emperor, same as you, lovey. Ain't our fault our home's low-g.' He turned away from her pointedly.

Haas groggily got to her feet. The room was crammed with longshanks. They had arrayed themselves as best they could around the walls, backs to the metal, long legs drawn up in front of them.

'Where are you from?' she asked. Haas was aware there were sanctioned sub-strains of humanity scattered around the galaxy, but that was as far as her knowledge went. On Terra any deviation from the norm was a mutation, and a mutant was a criminal by default.

'Orin's Well,' said Marast. 'Greenskins overran the planet and took thousands of us up here. Seems we're good for working on the moon. Most of it ain't got no gravity generators. Doesn't bother us as much as it bothers them. You?'

'You don't know where you are?'

Marast shook his head. 'Not a splinter of an idea. Been down here slaving for weeks now. Not many of us left.'

'Terra! You're in orbit over Terra!' She tapped the badge on her shoulder guard, much worn now, that marked her out as an arbitrator of the Imperial Palace, 149th Administrative District, General Oversight Division.

Marast's mouth opened wide in amazement. 'Terra?' He made the sign of the aquila over his chest. Murmurs went up from his freakish compatriots. A few reached out to touch her. She shook their hands off and stepped over their fragile-looking legs to the door.

'Don't do that!' hissed Marast. 'You'll have One Tooth in here on us!'

Something grunted outside. Haas threw herself against the wall as a bucket-jawed giant squinted into the room. One fang, a dirty beard. Her captor.

It banged on the door hard, making it shake in its mountings, and roared out a string of gruff alien words.

Marast crept to her side and pulled at her arm. 'Don't do that, don't talk, don't look them in the eye!' he said fearfully. 'If you do, they'll hurt you bad, might kill you, take you... take you through there!' He pointed at the wall.

'What's through there?' asked Haas, dreading the answer.

Marast winced. 'The meat pen.'

Haas could not help but look, her eyes drawn by a force outside of herself to the wall separating their holding pen from the room next door.

'I can't stay here. There must be a way out!' she said.

'Where to?' said Marast. 'Get out of that door and there are a million orks. Even if there weren't, where would you go? Walk to the surface and toss yourself off into space? Although that's better than the alternative, I suppose. But you can't. The only way we're getting off this moon is if someone comes and rescues us, and let me tell you something sad, lady arbitrator – no one's coming, not for the likes of us. You keep your head down, work hard, and they mostly leave you alone.'

'I won't. I'm going to get out of here,' whispered Haas.

Marast shook his head sadly. 'Not once you've seen the gate, you won't. It's hopeless.'

'Gate?'

'The place they come through. A flash of light, and they're there. As many orks as they need. There's no army in the galaxy that can stop them.'

In the boundary zone between the Oort cloud and the dwarf planets parading around the edge of the Sol System, space convulsed. Vile lightnings cracked around a puckering in the fabric of real space. With a silent scream, the universe tore.

Hundreds of warships arrowed into reality, diabolical vapours spilling off their glowing Geller fields. Behind them boiled the cauldron of the warp, a pit of madness none should cross. Reality sealed itself in a blinding flash of non-light, shuddered, and was still.

'High Marshal, my lord Chapter Master, we have arrived in the Sol System, praise be,' announced Bohemond's ship-master. Other reports followed.

'All decks report unproblematic translation.'

'Warp engines powering down.'

'Geller field deactivation in three, two, one. Geller field deactivated. All praise the Emperor, most holy Lord of Man.'

From the corner of his eye, Koorland saw Bohemond's twisted lips mouth the words silently along with his bondsmen.

The High Marshal of the Black Templars strode along the sweeping command deck of the *Abhorrence*. Fans of workstations spilled down from the command dais at the centre. A window of armourglass a dozen metres across filled the front of the deck, showing the blackness of space. At this far removed, Sol was merely a bright dot, hard to tell apart from any other star. Koorland stared at it, searching for the dim flicker that would mark out the location of Holy Terra.

'All Black Templars vessels, state arrival and status,' commanded Bohemond. 'Issachar, Quesadra, Thane. How do you fare?'

Cyber-constructs carrying holoprojectors swooped in

on Koorland and Bohemond's position, their projection gems bursting into life. The shoulders and heads of his fellow Chapter Masters assembled themselves in the air from striped pulses of laser light.

'All my vessels report zero casualties, no damage,' said Thane.

'The warp was unusually calm. Not a single vessel lost,' said Issachar.

'Fortune is with us,' said Quesadra.

'Fortune has nothing to do with it! It was the will of the Emperor. He knows we come to aid beleaguered Terra,' said Bohemond. 'Time check reports a warp transition of four days. Unprecedented. Your judgement was well founded, Brother Chapter Master Koorland.'

'I believe that was an apology, Brother Chapter Master,' said Quesadra quietly.

'My augur master has detected signs of recent fleet combat around Terra, minimal weapon discharge, and large informational exchange around the Martian noosphere. Where are the defence fleets? Why has Mars not mobilised its armies?' said Thane.

Koorland looked past the floating light spectres of his brothers.

'What are our orders, Imperial Fist?' said Issachar.

'The attack moon still orbits Terra,' said Koorland. 'We cannot let this insult stand. Brothers of the Last Wall, adopt attack formation,' he said. 'We make for the ork moon without delay. Send messages to Mars and Terra that we have come. As soon as we are close enough, open lithocast communications. We must learn how Terra can be held to ransom so easily.'

SIX

Dance's end

Lhaerial sat in the middle of a spherical room in a pool of brilliant light, bound by ankle, calf, and thigh to a high-backed chair. Her hands were imprisoned within a metal cylinder and pulled up over her back, so that she was forced forward, an uncomfortable position that seemed not to trouble her. Her mask had been taken from her, and her slender, pale-skinned face was visible, flawless but for a single black tear tattooed beneath each of her huge brown eyes. A male interrogator paced up and down in front of her, hands sweeping in expansive gestures, lips working hard. Veritus had the vox-link disengaged, and so Vangorich could not hear what he shouted at her. Instead they watched a pantomime: the angry enforcer, the apprehended villain.

'Shockingly young-looking, isn't she?' said Veritus. He and Vangorich stood behind a pane of psychically warded, one-way armourglass.

'Yes,' said Vangorich. He was fascinated by the eldar, never having seen one in the flesh before.

'And beautiful. I see it in your face, Vangorich, even in a cold-hearted killer like you.'

'I am not blind to beauty,' said Vangorich.

'Better to be!' said Veritus. 'Beauty is the cloak of many an enemy. Do not be deceived.' Veritus removed his hand from his chin and gestured at Lhaerial, the servo-motors aiding his ancient body burring softly in the quiet of the observation suite. 'She could be ten thousand years old. Only the most ancient of them show signs of ageing at all, and I hear that some never age a day. They are immortal, kept alive by black alien arts.'

'They are not immortal, inquisitor.'

Veritus spun on his heel, face darkening. Wienand stepped into the room, elegantly attired as always, her features set under her steel grey fringe. A few fresh lines had come to mark her face since the start of the crisis, yet still she seemed young to bear so much responsibility. The black matt metal door to the observation suite slid silently closed behind her. Vangorich glimpsed a pair of Inquisitorial storm troopers standing at guard outside. They had not been there when he and Veritus had arrived. Protection against Veritus.

'If you had thought to consult me, then you would be better informed, Lord Veritus,' said Wienand. 'If you weren't seeking my death.'

Veritus and Wienand stared at one another with hard eyes. Vangorich was hopeful of a rapprochement between the two, as matters were bad enough without the Inquisition falling to war with itself. But if there were to be one, there was little sign of it as yet.

'Yes,' said Veritus with a cold smile. 'They are your area of

expertise. I would expect nothing less than a deep understanding from someone who has so freely collaborated with
the enemies of the Imperium.'

'Not all xenos are our enemies, unless we choose to make
them so. They can be useful to us. Allies.'

Wienand stepped up to the glass to stand next to Veritus.

'You are tainted by your association, Wienand,' said Veritus. 'You should not be here. Should I be on my guard in
case you attempt to free her?'

'What would you do if I did? Never trust them, but do
not let hatred blind you. The eldar have aided us on many
occasions.'

'They are manipulators, they use us for their own ends,'
said Veritus.

'Then we must manipulate them back!' said Wienand.
'Better that than open war.'

'Is it?' said Veritus. The inquisitors stared fixedly into the
room, neither looking at the other as they argued. Vangorich
was trapped in the middle, witness to a sour lovers' tiff.

Vangorich held up his hands. 'Please. Stop.'

The inquisitors took his rebuke without comment, to
Vangorich's relief. Even he couldn't fight his way out of the
Inquisitorial Fortress. But there was plenty of time for one
or both of them to turn against him, he thought. 'Wienand,
it is good to see you again.'

'You too, Drakan, although I think very little of the company you are keeping.'

'Can we not concentrate on the matter at hand here?' said
Vangorich wearily. 'What's an assassination attempt or two
between friends?'

'So speaks the Assassin,' said Wienand.

'He has a point, Wienand,' snarled Veritus, then calmed. He turned to face Wienand but did not look her in the eye, instead gazing fixedly over her shoulder. 'Maybe I acted hastily, but things had come to a shocking pass and–'

'You did not agree with my actions as Inquisitorial Representative, very good. You had recourse to options other than murder and usurpation!' she interrupted.

'We had no time!' said Veritus. 'You would not have gone quietly, and we would have fought as stupidly as the fools in the Senate, jockeying for power as the Imperium burned around us.'

'So my death was a matter of expediency? How very comforting.'

'Yes.' Veritus sighed. 'I am old, Wienand. So much older than you. I have seen so much stupidity. I could not take a chance.'

'And now I am stupid.' She aggressively sought out his eyes with her own. 'Did you not think just to ask? No?'

Veritus' aged lips pressed thin, going grey.

'Tell me then, Representative Veritus. How goes your management of the crisis?' said Wienand.

Vangorich cleared his throat. 'This glass, it is psychically blocked, is it not?'

The inquisitors looked over his head.

'Really,' he said, 'I have spent many long years perfecting an air of unimportance, I am used to being ignored, but this is too much. Answer me! Veritus? Is this glass warded?'

'Yes, yes of course,' snapped Veritus. 'Why?'

'Because if you stopped glaring at Wienand there, you'd

see that our prisoner is looking right at you, and she finds something amusing.'

Wienand shook her head dismissively and returned her attention to the prisoner. 'Have you actually spoken to her yet, Veritus, or did you just plan on killing her too?'

'Not yet!' said Vangorich lightly. 'How about we attempt that right now? There is no time like the present.'

Veritus cleared his throat. A phlegmy, old man's sound. 'Very well,' he said.

Wienand, Vangorich and Veritus entered the room, the inquisitors still eyeing each other warily. The interrogator ceased his questioning, bowed and withdrew without a word.

'At last you come out!' said the prisoner. 'So pathetic are your attempts at masking that any child of my people could better them without effort.'

The three humans lined up in front of the prisoner. She stared at them contemptuously. The removal of her mask had brought a marked change in her manner. She had become more aloof, more cautious, more direct in speech, but it had only sharpened her defiance.

'It is time to discuss your message,' said Wienand.

'As I told your friends, I come in peace.'

'I have a strange appreciation of the word myself,' said Vangorich.

'You are a murderer. I smell blood on you,' Lhaerial said.

'Quite,' said Vangorich. He found the anger in her quite beguiling. 'My point is, arriving armed and shooting is not covered by any definition of peace.'

'Would you have listened?' she said.

'Probably not,' said Vangorich.

'Drakan,' said Wienand, 'this is our prisoner.'

'Of course, of course, please, inquisitors. Inquire.'

'You are a psyker?' said Veritus.

'And what is that?' Lhaerial said.

'A witch, a seer.'

She nodded. 'A seer of the shadows.'

'Then let it be known I am warded against your powers,' said Veritus.

'I know your mind regardless,' said the eldar.

'Tell me of your mission,' said Wienand.

'I already have,' said Lhaerial.

'Again,' said Wienand. 'To us.'

'I should repeat myself? And then you will ask me again, and again, and you will attempt to hurt me. You are so primitive. I do not know why Eldrad Ulthran wishes to save you. The galaxy would be a cleaner place were you to be exterminated.'

'You lack the power for that now,' said Wienand, surprisingly gently. 'And I think when your kind did have that might, something stayed your hand.'

Lhaerial cocked an eyebrow and gave a sudden, savage smile. 'Maybe. Doubtless you think our positions reversed? You cannot hurt me. I am Cegorach's.'

'She speaks of one of their gods,' explained Wienand.

'Do not be so sure, eldar,' said Veritus dangerously. Wienand held up her hand behind her irritably.

'Tell us,' said Wienand. 'The last time.'

Lhaerial closed her eyes. They were so big, thought Vangorich.

'I was to deliver a message to the Emperor, not to you.'

'Tell us what was in this message. We are the representatives of His will,' said Wienand. 'The Emperor cannot be spoken to, He is entombed.'

'You think we do not know this? Eldrad Ulthran, greatest seer of all, entrusted me with this task. I was chosen because I am a seer, I have opened my mind, the old ways are mine. I do not fear She Who Thirsts.'

'He cannot be reached even psychically,' said Wienand. 'It has been tried. You would have died. You must tell us.'

'What was the message? A threat?' challenged Veritus.

'Foolish mon-keigh!' hissed Lhaerial Rey. Her eyes snapped open. 'No threat! The Emperor and the farseer are known to each other. Though they long diverged from friendship, they are not yet opposed. Your dead Emperor is the only hope, for us all, man and eldar alike. This current crisis will pass. The roar of the ork will subside, while the real threat grows. You, the one who calls himself Veritus, you know this to be the truth. I know what you have seen.'

Veritus stepped back, appalled.

'You are fools to yourselves,' spat Lhaerial. 'You are right, old one, and she is right. There is more than one answer to every question. Listen! The ork moon will not last here.'

'How can you be so sure?'

'I bring news also of a gift. A force of your Space Marines have gathered in great number, and make their way here. Even now, they pass the red world of this system. Eldrad Ulthran and the seers of Ulthwé worked long and hard to quell the storms roused in the Othersea by the orks, the better that they might come to you. This gift is given freely, because we hope with all our hearts you shall prevail over the ork.

'Listen to our pleas. Do not let the orks distract you, nor any other threat arising from the temporal realm. The gods of the Othersea will not stop until this galaxy is their plaything. The threat they pose is millions of cycles old, the actions of your Warmaster but the latest act in a war that has raged since the time of the old races. For the lifespan of stars my people have opposed them. You are naive if you think Chaos defeated. I have been sent with this one message – do not neglect the Dark Gods, for it will mean the annihilation of us all.'

'Do you suggest that only mankind might save the galaxy?' said Veritus wonderingly.

Lhaerial shifted her gaze to Veritus, and her hard eyes made him flinch as if she saw something in his mind and reflected it back upon him. 'The idea appeals to your vanity? You were correct in what you were saying, through there. You are a tool to us. Our people ruled the stars when this world was ruled by reptiles. Many came against us – the soulless ones, the krork at the apex of their might, in comparison to which this latest folly is laughable, the cythor and a thousand other races so terrible your intellects could not contemplate them. Even your own ancestors and their unliving legions at the so-called height of their mastery. We defeated them all.

'To you we seem a sorry remnant, a ragged glory fading into the void, but we are not yet extinct, inquisitor. What is a few thousand cycles of weakness when set against millions of power? You fell yourselves, your empire is a pathetic

mockery of what your kind once had. Mark my words well –
unlike you we shall be mighty once again. We would prefer
it if there were still a galaxy to rule when we are ready to
return.'

Wienand pursed her lips and shook her head regretfully.

'You do yourself no favours,' she said. 'I am trying to help
you.'

A fanatical light shone from Veritus' eyes as he looked
at the eldar. 'Now that is a threat,' he said. 'Listen to me,
alien. I know the truth of it, awful as it is. There is one path
to peace, and that is when every last world is under the
hegemony of mankind.'

Lhaerial smiled. Her teeth were very small, perfectly white.
'You are mistaken. You safeguard our heritage, until the time
comes for the Empire of Ten Million Suns to rise once again.
For that reason alone we vouchsafe your continued existence. The Primordial Annihilator is our common enemy.
Our kind coexisted before the fall. We have no quarrel with
you.'

Veritus stepped menacingly close to the eldar.

'The Debari incident, the Veridanium massacre, the fall
of Outremer, the burning of Choidenmirn.' He counted
off atrocities on golden metal fingers. 'All these were per-
petrated by your species against ours, and in the last five
hundred years.'

'Not all of my kind are of good heart, just as not all of
yours are.'

Veritus laughed. 'You claim to represent the world-ship
of Ulthwé? All of those were actions of that faction against
the Imperium!'

Lhaerial managed to shrug, despite her binding. 'The worlds of Ulthwé that you trespass upon, doubtless they thought the punishment necessary.'

'Then how can we possibly trust you?' shouted Veritus.

Lhaerial looked into the ancient inquisitor's face. 'How can we possibly trust you? We only have each other, for now at least. We can stand apart and die alone, or we might persist together.'

'This is intolerable!' snapped Veritus.

'Calm yourself, Veritus,' said Wienand. 'Listen to what she is saying – she is right. We must listen to her. If they truly wanted to harm the Emperor, they would have come against us differently, if it were in their power to do so. I believe her. She speaks the truth.'

'You are corrupted by their influence!' said Veritus. 'Van der Deckart told me all about your actions on Antagonis in concert with these creatures. They are fundamentally untrustworthy. Your dealings with them are grounds enough for execution!'

'On whose authority?' said Wienand.

'I am the Inquisitorial Representative,' said Veritus. 'On my authority.'

'You are the Inquisitorial Representative by nefarious means. I am the incumbent, you are the impostor. And we are not in the halls of government now. We are among our own kind. You are not popular in this fortress, Veritus. I have many supporters here.'

'I have many also,' said Veritus warningly.

'I should kill you now.'

'Stop!' Vangorich stepped between them. 'Is this really the

time?' he said, looking at the prisoner. Lhaerial Rey's head hung, unconcerned at the humans' conversation.

'Oh, this is the perfect time for this conversation,' said Veritus. 'The eldar is going nowhere, and this room is among the most heavily warded in all the Fortress, a good venue for the most private of affairs.' His hand rested against his pistol.

'Don't! Don't draw that! Listen to yourselves!' said a pained Vangorich. He pinched the bridge of his nose and breathed through his teeth. 'Ordinarily I would have no qualms if the two of you wished to pit the Inquisition against itself. Your agency has interrupted legitimate operations of mine so many times I have lost my patience with it. A reorganisation would do it and me a world of good.'

'We impose the will of the Emperor, Drakan,' said Wienand. 'Our word is law.'

'And I exist to ensure that people who say such things as a matter of habit do not take matters into their own hands. Isn't it nice that we can all get on so well together?' Vangorich said drily. 'We do need to get on with each other. Frankly, you two and I are the only ones who seem to be keeping their head in all of this mess. Can you not put your differences aside? The future of the Imperium depends on it. Is it really that inconceivable that you both might be right? That Veritus here is correct to be wary of the alien.'

Veritus began to speak, but Vangorich raised his voice and spoke over him.

'And that Wienand is right in the utility of the xenos? Neither of these viewpoints are essentially contradictory. Perhaps, indeed, it is time to consider a certain amount of specialisation? Take a lead from my temples. One must

select the correct tool for the job. This is a big galaxy – no one man or woman can hope to be fit for every task, even if they carry the Emperor's seal. In your division you are behaving no less blindly or selfishly than the High Lords.'

Veritus worked his jaw. Wienand stared down her nose at him.

'So,' said Vangorich. 'Who's first?'

'Very well,' said Wienand. 'I shall agree to a detente.'

'Veritus?' said Vangorich.

Veritus sneered. 'And hand back power to you, I suppose? Your record so far has been pitiful, Wienand.'

'On the contrary. You shall remain as the Inquisitorial Representative,' said Wienand. 'My return will raise questions. Open signs of dissent within our ranks will weaken our position. Matters are too delicate to confuse further with my return. The Inquisition must present a united front, outwardly at least. I shall be able to act more freely against the High Lords if I remain dead.'

Vangorich smiled in relief, interleaved his fingers and cracked his knuckles.

'Well then!' he said.

'Surprised, Veritus? You see, my lord,' said Wienand, 'it is not only you who has the interests of the Imperium at heart.'

'Excellent!' said Vangorich. 'We must begin work immediately.' He ushered them towards the door.

'Be hasty,' said the shadowseer. 'Already the Primordial Annihilator works against you.'

Vangorich got one final look at Lhaerial Rey before the door sealed, locking her away forever.

SEVEN

A conversation with Terra

During their voyage across the Sol System, Koorland found his few moments of peace in the practice cages. With Issachar he sparred constantly, both of them guests of Bohemond. The physical exertion of combat pushed aside his grief and his anger. When not fighting, the lords of the Chapters conferred and feasted, making their plans against the orks.

The Last Wall made all speed through the Sol System, sailing past mighty Jupiter and its glowering storm spots, on towards the asteroid belt and past it to the inner planets. From fleeing mercantile craft they first received detailed news of the situation at Terra, and of the disastrous Proletarian Crusade.

The Sol System was ordinarily alive with shipping travelling from the Mandeville point to Terra. The Last Wall saw few vessels. Those ships that had come to the cradle of mankind had aborted their journeys, and lurked unsurely around the outer planets. The captains of the ships and the

lords of minor colonies around the gas giants relayed further details. The moon had arrived at Terra unopposed, they said, crushing the throneworld's orbital defences without trouble. The Navy was mostly absent. When the Crusade had been called, the minor Imperial Navy presence held back while millions of Imperial citizens were slaughtered. Worse still, the ships of Mars remained in port, the red world's armies mustered but inactive. Astropathic messages to both Terra and Mars went unanswered.

Koorland's outrage grew. During the hours of swift travel from the Mandeville point to the inner system he remained in the cages. His sword clashed off Issachar's twin axes. He fought instinctively, mind elsewhere. Several questions troubled him, and the answer to them all was more troubling still – the High Lords, the High Lords, the High Lords.

He grunted hard, and swung at Issachar. The Excoriator dodged.

'My lords.'

Koorland drove another hard attack at Issachar, all his anger and frustration behind it.

'My lords!'

Issachar caught Koorland's blow upon crossed axes.

'A messenger,' said Issachar, nodding past their locked weapons. He and Koorland were stripped to the waist. Issachar's torso was as scarified as his face, his flesh a coded manual to the rituals of his Chapter.

Koorland stepped back. Sweat poured off them both. A Black Templars bondsman stood by the doors, framed by the cage bars.

'The High Lords have made contact, my lords,' said the

bondsman. He wore the weapons of a warrior, and had the physique to match. His attitude to Koorland was deferential without servility. There was pride in the hearts of the Black Templars' men; they did not creep about as the servants of some Chapters did.

'No news from Mars?' said Koorland. He wiped down his face and naked torso with a towel handed to him by an arming servitor, and stepped out from the practice cage.

'Alas, we have heard nothing from them, my lord.'

'Continue our attempts to raise them. Have your astropaths and vox-officers make the implication the Last Wall may alter course to put into orbit around the forge world and investigate their silence. That will focus the tech-priests' attention,' said Koorland. 'Have my armour prepared. I will speak with the High Lords garbed for war.'

'Shall I inform my liege Bohemond?'

'I shall speak to this representative alone,' said Koorland.

'My lord,' said the bondsman, and departed.

'If the High Lords contact us, we can rest easy that there is at least authority still upon Terra,' said Issachar.

'Yes, but whose?' said Koorland. 'And if the old authority, how effective can it be? The High Lords have proved nothing but their own incompetence.'

'You are learning, Chapter Master Koorland.'

While in the arming chamber Bohemond had provided him, Koorland was informed that the representative of the High Lords was now present via lithocast. Koorland did not hurry. Arming servitors and bondsmen clad him in his armour, polished now but still bearing the marks of

the conflict on Ardamantua. While the men worked silent around him, bolting him into his battleplate, he thought on what he must say to the lords of all the Imperium. Politics. How he loathed them, all the worse as he lacked the detail to make an adequate tactical plan. Idle fantasies of usurping them and replacing their corrupt rule with that of the Space Marines played through his mind. But Space Marines were no less fallible than mortal men, and far more dangerous for the belief many of them had in their own rectitude. The galaxy had suffered enough already because of transhuman arrogance. He chastised himself inwardly. Issachar's sentiments were infectious. He could not succumb to them.

The last clasp of his armour fastened with a snap. The bondsmen oiled Koorland's hair, set a cloak of rich red velvet about his shoulders, and he departed for the Chamber of Audience, high up on the *Abhorrence*'s superstructure. As befitted its purpose as a tool of diplomacy, the chamber was cavernous, possessing enough holoprojectors to accommodate the remote meetings of many hundreds of men. Only one awaited him, the slight phantom of an unremarkable man in the room's centre, his full-size lithocast eerily lifelike.

'My lord, my apologies for keeping you,' said Koorland. The room swallowed his voice whole. His footsteps echoed sharply from the ornate walls.

The representative of the High Lords waved away the apology. He was plainly dressed, small.

'These are trying times. I have not been waiting long. Rather, it is my own eagerness to speak with you that brings me to the lithocast chamber ahead of you, Second Captain Koorland.'

'I am Chapter Master now,' said Koorland.

'Ah,' said the man. His face expressed his concern, the long scar cutting across it wrinkling oddly. 'Your losses were grave, we understand. Tell me, were there other survivors?'

'They are dead,' said Koorland icily. 'You do not understand, I think. They are all dead, every one of my brothers. I am the last of the Imperial Fists. When I fall, the Chapter shall be no more.'

'All of them are dead?' said the man softly.

'All.'

The man nodded. 'I feared as much. On hearing of your survival, some of my colleagues were more hopeful that others might have been retrieved, but...' His demeanour changed. 'We are forgetting ourselves, Chapter Master. I have yet to introduce myself. I am Drakan Vangorich, head of the Officio Assassinorum, and one of the High Lords of Terra, though sadly not one of the Twelve.'

'You? You are the Lord of Assassins?' said Koorland.

'You cannot hide your incredulity. That is understandable.' The man's slight pleasure offended Koorland. 'You have yet to grasp the diplomatic niceties of your new role. I do not look like a master of murderers, and intentionally so. If I looked like death himself, I would be performing my job poorly, would I not?'

'Why have you been chosen to speak with me?' Koorland's mind raced. Battle. He must see this as battle. There were tactical considerations in the choice of his words. Koorland chose to be blunt. 'Is this a warning?'

'Yes. Yes, I suppose there is a warning in what I'm saying to you, Chapter Master,' said Vangorich amiably. 'But not the kind you are thinking of. Doubtless you believe my communication is meant to convey the power of the High Lords. At my command are killers who would tax and quite probably kill even you, should I command it. And it is true, the arrival of your fleet has caused as much consternation as it has celebration. But my warning is not of that sort. I ask that you pay attention to what I said regarding my appearance. Things are so very rarely as they seem.'

'You are speaking obtusely.'

'I really am not,' said Vangorich.

'Then tell me plainly, what is the High Lords' message?'

'There's the crux of it. I am reasonably confident the High Lords' message would be that you stay far away from Terra. They'd say this because you will provoke the orks, who for the four days since their ambassador was sent to us have done nothing. In fairness, the High Lords may genuinely fear provocation. What they really fear, however, is the threat to their power your – several thousand, is it? – Space Marines pose. Even at this late hour, they scheme still, and you are forcing them to act in concert. Nothing is more apt to form a concord among them than a challenge to their power from within the Imperium. A shame they do not categorise this ork invasion similarly. Terror is at the forefront of their minds, but behind it self-interest, ambition and envy still slide over one another, poisonous as serpents.'

'I do not understand,' said Koorland. 'I requested, politely, that you speak plainly. Do not make me demand.'

Vangorich pointed at Koorland somewhat impishly. 'A little steel I see there, Chapter Master. Good. We are sorely in need of a man with steel. You must also learn a certain flexibility of mind. You see, I am not speaking to you on behalf of the High Lords at all. I am currently at the Inquisitorial Headquarters. I am afraid I am very much on a frolic of my own.'

'I was expecting instruction. Plans. Disposition of the enemy.'

'Very commendable. Instruction I can manage. I have with me one of my colleagues, Veritus, the Inquisitorial Representative to the Senatorum Imperialis, and one of the High Twelve. He and I unfortunately do not constitute a quorum, but Veritus has something our fellows in the Senatorum lack. He speaks with the voice of the Emperor.'

The hololith blinked. A second figure appeared on the focusing platform alongside the one projecting Vangorich. An indefinably ancient man, encased in a suit of golden power armour.

'I am Veritus, the Inquisitorial Representative, and one of the High Twelve,' said the newcomer. 'Will you heed my command, Chapter Master Koorland? Will you obey the word of the Emperor Himself?'

Koorland's relief at having made contact with some authority was undermined by the uneasy feeling a trap was opening before him. The Chapters were autonomous but even they could not deny a direct order from a High Lord. He must tread carefully. 'State your orders, inquisitor.'

'By the power vested in me,' said Veritus, 'the High Lords command that you bring your fleet immediately to Terra and smash the attack moon out of the sky.'

'And why do you think we have come here, inquisitor? Has the Imperium become so divided that the sight of a fleet of

Space Marines in response to a direct threat within the holy system of Sol inspires fear, and not relief? Our intention is to destroy the orks,' said Koorland. 'It is our only purpose.'

'Then our aims accord,' said Veritus guardedly.

'Well, that was very dramatic,' said Vangorich. 'But there is some business to attend to. You will require help, lord Chapter Master. You must go to Mars, and winkle Fabricator General Kubik out from his hiding place. Set his feet on the path to war. The man sits in his palace surrounded by one of the mightiest armies in the galaxy, and he does nothing. We will advise you in what you must say to him.' Vangorich glanced at Veritus. 'But first, it is time to tell you exactly what has transpired since the tragedy at Ardamantua. Steady yourself – you will not be pleased by what I have to say.'

EIGHT

The calculation of suspicion

Kubik addressed Koorland from the heart of the diagnostiad, the clicking mind of Mars. A kilometre-wide sphere excavated from the ground in untold ages past, its sides were a hive of thousands of individual cells, each containing the body of a magos wired directly into the Martian world-core. Their whispering never stopped. Once placed inside a cell, a magos left only when his unnaturally long life was worked out. Dark patches on the wall marked out an expired follower of the Omnissiah, like dead elements on a pict screen. Sometimes they might go for months without notice until servitor teams carefully cleared brown bones, failed cybernetics and ruined robes from the cavity, and prepared it for a new occupant. It was a networked mind, far more powerful than any cogitator in the galaxy. Retaining but a fragment of their individuality, the magi became one in thought and intent; the diagnostiad had known no dissension within itself for hundreds of years.

There were few honours higher in the priesthood than to

be elevated to the diagnostiad. To join the world-engine at the heart of the Martian empire was to commune with the Omnissiah himself.

The office of Fabricator General was one of those few higher honours. Surrounded by thousands trapped in the ecstasy of mechanical undeath, it was an honour Kubik preferred.

Kubik's throne was a mighty affair, replete with data sockets, cogitator interface points, servo-skull docks and other, more esoteric devices that provided Kubik with a direct link to the mind of Mars. Backed by a giant brazen plaque depicting the machina opus, the throne occupied a dais raised on a spine in the heart of the sphere, a tall needle alight with the sparkings of the Motive Force, and set with the polished bones and preserved cybernetica of his predecessors. Like the arcane knowledge of the tech-priests, Kubik's throne was founded on the bones of the past.

At the Fabricator General's insistence, Koorland spoke with Kubik from a private lithocast chamber aboard the *Abhorrence*. A perfect, life-size image of the Chapter Master was projected by his throne in a manner that meant only Kubik and the diagnostiad could see him. No other sentient was present in the sphere, and yet secrecy reigned even there. The instinct to hoard knowledge was the most powerful a tech-priest possessed. Their mastery of technology was second only to their paranoia.

'Well met, Chapter Master Koorland. Your return to Sol is timely. Without your arrival, Terra would surely be lost.' Kubik selected a near-human voice from his editicore

recollections, a rich, commanding voice, suggestive of mas-
culinity and confidence. Entirely unlike Kubik's original
voice, now hundreds of years lost.

'Greetings to you, Lord of Mars,' said Koorland, and bowed.
'We, the brothers of the Last Wall, come before you to ask
for your aid and your wisdom.'

The Space Marine was being deferential. Kubik wondered
who had schooled him.

'We move immediately upon the attack moon,' said Koorland. 'Surprise is our most potent weapon. We will fall on
them, and smash them from the skies.'

'So thought Juskina Tull, and her Proletarian Crusade
ended in disaster.' Kubik's sub-processors kept his voice
neutral, injecting elements of superiority, irony and calm
into the vox-output.

'We are the hammer of the Emperor, not a desperate rabble. We shall destroy the orks.'

'I can only applaud your confidence, Chapter Master, but
I insist on caution.'

'And I can only query your lack of action,' said Koorland.

'It is no mystery,' said Kubik. 'Our ground forces are substantial here on Mars, but our fleets are not suitable for
actions of this kind. We have few vessels within the system
in any case. To throw our lot in with Juskina Tull would have
resulted in the loss of valuable military units that might be
better used elsewhere.'

'What of your weapons arrays, your machines of great
art? Surely there is something capable of destroying the
moon upon Mars.'

'Indeed,' said Kubik. 'And using any of the Greater

Weapons would have posed unconscionable risks to Holy Terra. Would you have us destroy the throneworld to save it?'

Koorland gave Kubik a look the Fabricator General found unreadable. He queried the diagnostiad via mind shunt.

<Voice analysis and facial muscle configurations suggest he is close to speaking freely,> spoke the diagnostiad into Kubik's mind. It addressed him with a single voice. <He believes you to be dissembling. We calculate a ninety per cent probability that he has been in contact with others within the system. Primary suspects – Grand Master Vangorich, Inquisitor Veritus.>

'Let us not point the finger, Chapter Master,' said Kubik. 'This war has taken us all by surprise. You have a good chance of success. In aiding you I will not be casting my military away needlessly, so you I shall aid. That was your intention in contacting me, yes? To ask for my help, and not cast aspersion and accusation?'

Koorland nodded curtly. 'Yes, my lord. That was my intention.'

'Good. Five regiments of skitarii will accompany you, and attendant support. I will pledge also seven cohorts of the Legio Cybernetica. The Basilikon Astra will transport them, and provide heavy supportive fire. Alone, or in support of the Merchant Fleets, our warships would have stood little chance. With your battlefleet, they can operate within acceptable parameters of survival.'

'I desire to speak with Phaeton Laurentis and Eldon Urquidex,' said Koorland. 'They are known to me, and I would confer with them.'

'Urquidex, Laurentis? I am not familiar with them. One

moment please.' Kubik made a show of calling up their information. 'Ah yes, minor biologians. Unfortunately, both magi are occupied with other duties.'

'Another time, perhaps,' said Koorland. 'You have our thanks, Fabricator General. While the Imperium stands together, it shall not fall.'

'Mars will not allow that to happen. We are united, as always.'

<He suspects you lie,> whispered the diagnostiad.

'When will your forces be ready?' asked Koorland.

'Chapter Master, I called the Taghmata of Mars weeks ago in anticipation of reinforcement. Our military is already prepared to sail as soon as I give the word. You insult me and the oaths of fealty and alliance Mars holds in sacred compact with Holy Terra. We have stood ready to sail to Terra's aid since the very first. We could not act alone, nor would we support the fool's crusade called by Juskina Tull.' Kubik stood from his throne, mechadendrites and other, subtler supplementary limbs waving in displeasure.

'You have my apologies, Fabricator General,' said Koorland. 'No implication was meant. Your aid is generous, and will save the lives of many of the sons of Dorn.'

'Transmit me your marshalling coordinates. I will despatch the Taghmata, and place the Prime under your direct command. I have only one request.'

'That is, my lord?'

'Any and all materiel and technology taken in the battle must be collected by my subjects, and delivered here to Mars.'

'For what purpose?' asked Koorland.

'Its study is vital to the defeat of the orks.'

'I will agree to this, in exchange for all information pertaining to the ork threat you have already gathered.'

'We have provided what we know to the Senatorum,' said Kubik smoothly.

'There are explorator fleets all over the Imperium,' said Koorland. 'Many of your forge worlds have been attacked. I have seen some of the intelligence you have gathered. It seems a little... thin.'

'It is all we have,' said Kubik. 'Delivery of materiel will speed our analysis. We shall share what we learn when we have learnt it.'

Koorland stared a long moment at the Fabricator General. 'Very well, but we shall oversee the transfer.'

'Agreed,' said Kubik.

'We will speak again soon, on the day of our victory.'

Koorland's image vanished as Kubik cut the link. The whispering of the diagnostiad members rose and fell like the rush of wind in the leaves of a forest. Kubik took to his throne again, and commanded it to descend. Gracefully it sank away, bringing Kubik to rest upon the only flat surface in the sphere, and the only part free of the cavities of the diagnostiad's cells – a platform a hundred metres across, a raised road of Martian bronze leading across it to a huge pair of doors, guarded by a phalanx of stooped cyber-constructs. Kubik glided out of his throne. The doors opened before him. Outside stood the primary members of the Synod of Mars, waiting on his orders. Bowing profusely, they took his commands.

* * *

Eldon Urquidex was marched alongside Magos Laurentis up the Channel of Motivational Energies as Performed by the Flesh, a broad processional way laid out in mimicry of the internal workings of a cogitator's logic boards. They were deep within the forge temple of Olympus Mons. Passages left at irregular intervals, each one guarded by bio-constructs and barred by heavy grilles known as the Gates of Logic.

The Channel was the largest road in a three-dimensional labyrinth, and the main route taken by supplicants to the Synod of Mars. The edifice had been constructed aeons ago during Old Night by a Fabricator General of questionable sanity, the legacy of costly experiments to mimic the ineffable deductive powers of pure energy through the medium of humanity. Techna-liturgia moving around the circuit were supposed to operate in a manner similar to the sub-atomic particles of the holy Motive Force. It had not of course worked, but where it had failed as a computational device, it succeeded as art, and remained a sacred place.

The Channel bored through the mountain in a las-straight line to the audience chamber of the Fabricator General, and Urquidex was worried.

Urquidex's mechanical face was misleading. Behind the steel and the telescopic eye stalks lurked a very human brain. Not so long ago, Urquidex would have welcomed an appointment with Kubik as an opportunity to secure advancement with the Synod. Manipulation, flattery, spurious logic – these tools were Urquidex's to deploy as easily as the fine manipulators on his additional limbs. That was before he became a traitor. Fear chilled the fluids in the tubes of his augmetics. Urquidex had worked himself to the centre of Kubik's plans, and had come to disagree with them entirely. With news of the Last Wall's arrival at Sol, and their dash for Terra, Kubik's intelligence core and native brain alike would be slaved entirely to political scheming. It would take the slightest misstep to expose Urquidex. What small patches of skin remained to him were slick with the unpleasant excretions of anxiety.

The heavy tread of Kubik's cybernetic guardians rang ominously on the metal plates of the Channel. Everything Urquidex saw, his nerves imbued with a sinister aspect. Servo-skulls and vat-constructs darting through the air became spies following his every movement. The chants of magi and electro-priests droning from the factory-chapels and techno-basilicae carried counter-melodies of accusation. The hisses and whines of holy manufacturing processes barely concealed their contempt for him. Laurentis, his emotions so heavily circumscribed by the surgery necessary to save his life after Ardamantua, lurched along placidly on his tripedal motive assembly, the thoughts whirring through his rebuilt brain secret from all.

Urquidex was no Ultima Mechanista, wishing away his humanity; for him and the members of his sub-cult, balance was to be sought between mechanical and organic. For was not the flesh nothing but the wet machinery of the Omnissiah? Finding such a balance was a cause of much worry to Urquidex. He thought back to Ardamantua, torn between the cold logic of the *Subservius'* mission and the horror he had experienced at the annihilation of the Imperial Fists.

Ruminating on that weakness, he envied Laurentis his new-found detachment.

Too soon they came to Kubik's audience chamber. The doors were a pair of cogs set in series, one bearing a skull, the other a mechanical face: the machina opus split into two wholes. The cyber-constructs stopped and slammed their power glaives into the metal floor.

With mouthless voices they announced the magi's arrival. 'Magi Biologis Eldon Urquidex and Phaeton Laurentis request audience with his high logician the Fabricator General of Mars.'

Urquidex found that rich. There had been no request, they had been summoned. He would rather be anywhere than in Kubik's presence today. Did Kubik know? Had that giant intellect uncovered his involvement with the agents of the Officio Assassinorum?

The doors rolled apart in opposite directions. Urquidex and Laurentis were ushered in. The audience chamber was designed to intimidate. On his best days, Urquidex found the vast space, crisscrossed with giant, crackling power conduits and humming with data-streams emanating from the diagnostiad, to be unnerving, and today was not one of his best days. Urquidex steadied himself and put his emotional feeds on temporary hold, redirecting his thought processes through the far steadier mechanisms of his intelligence core.

'O mighty and most wise Fabricator General Kubik! Prime of primes, artisan without compare,' said Urquidex, spreading his multiple limbs and executing a complex obeisance. 'I am your humble servant. State your bidding, and I shall comply to the letter, without the error of signal loss or personal interpretation.'

Laurentis said nothing, but executed an awkward three-legged curtsey, his single organic eye blinking incongruously in the centre of his facial mechanisms.

Kubik sat in a high-backed, ovoid chair that floated a metre above the ground on a snapping grav-field. The dusty smell of high-energy discharge washed out from it as he floated forward to stop not far from the two biologians, the repulsor unit of the chair buffeting at their robes.

'Magos Biologis Eldon Urquidex, Magos Biologis Phaeton Laurentis.'

'Prime of primes, alpha of alphas,' said Urquidex.

Laurentis said nothing.

'Tell me,' said Kubik. 'What do you know of Second Captain Koorland of the Imperial Fists, lately returned to this system?'

Urquidex's mechanical body parts sagged with relief. 'Whatever you wish to know, Lord of Mars.'

Kubik's chair turned, its energy field spitting, and he performed a slow circuit around the magi.

'Laurentis first, you spent much time with him on Ardamantua.'

'He was kind,' said Laurentis, his vocal modulator thoughtful. 'Honourable.' Laurentis paused. 'Fabricator General, it is often wise in such circumstances as these, where mismatch exists between the relative hierarchical status of two participants in an exchange, to provide an opinion not necessarily held by the responder. To give informative discourse couched in the subjective language that tallies with the result the interlocutor wishes to hear. I calculate you wish to hear the bad, but I cannot voice it. He saved my life.'

'Speak the truth. Flattery compromises logic,' said Kubik.

'I will say nothing against him,' said Laurentis. 'He is, in common parlance, a hero. After my transformation, he threatened Magos Urquidex with violence should additional damaging circumstance befall me.'

'And why is this remarkable?' asked Kubik. 'The primary purpose of the Adeptus Astartes is to safeguard and promote the persistence of the human race. They are made to be that way, as predictable as the energy output of a lasgun.'

'It is possible he was following his indoctrinative programming,' conceded Laurentis. 'But I believe he genuinely wished to help me personally.'

'Intriguing. An altruist. An uncertain modifier to my calculations.'

'There is more. He was also... sad,' said Laurentis, as if struggling to recall what the word meant.

'And you, Urquidex? State your initial observations and hypothetical deductions.'

'He was most persuasive,' said Urquidex unctuously. 'Unafraid to offer violence to further his aims.' Urquidex remembered being slammed into a wall. Most unpleasant. 'I found him driven. He will not be easily controlled.'

Kubik's subsidiary vocalisers made a dry clacking laugh. His primary voice remained thoughtful and cold. 'Do not second-guess my intentions, Urquidex.'

'I only think on the progress of the Grand Experiment, and how the arrival of the Last Wall will affect that progress,' said Urquidex.

'You and I are not dissimilar,' said Kubik. 'We are both biologians, even if our specialisations differ. Our creed is a self-evident truth – to abandon humanity entirely is a self-defeating exercise. Logic is a tool best utilised by a thinking, feeling organism, not an end unto itself. The end is knowledge, not logic as some of our brethren believe. Logic gives us a framework to understanding, but it does not provide insight. Without insight I could never have become Fabricator General nor could I survive the political processes of the Senatorum Imperialis. Logic is not the only mode of thought necessary to true communion with the Omnissiah. The flesh is weak, but the machine on its own is weak also.

'Let the cults of expunging strip away their humanity and decry us as *modus unbecoming*. We must never forget the even split upon the Omnissiah's own sigil, skull and cybernetic. A sentiment the magi of the Ordo Biologis can only agree with, is that not so, Laurentis? Before your unfortunate wounding, you had few augmentations.'

'A choice I made to remain better attuned to subtleties of biology, Fabricator General,' said Laurentis. 'I have lost so much to the orks. I see more clearly now, but what was taken from me was not given willingly. I cannot imagine giving up so much of gross human feeling as a conscious act. What little emotion remains is coloured throughout with regret.'

'Your skills as a dialogian remain. Do you still possess the necessary knowledge and mental subroutines to act as an effective translator?'

'I remain first and foremost of the xenology sub-order,'

said Laurentis. 'Linguistic expression is a part of my ability, not the whole.'

'Nevertheless, it is your linguistic ability I enquire after,' said Kubik. Upbraiding so heavily cybernised an adept as Laurentis for pedantry was pointless.

'My linguistic skills are two-point-three-four per cent more efficient than they were,' said Laurentis. 'What I have lost in instinctive appreciation for the modes of speech, I have gained in rapid pattern recognition.'

Kubik swept around the magi again. 'Then you are to report after this meeting to Artisan Trajectorae Augus Van Auken at Pavonis Mons. There is a new project of grave importance being undertaken, vital to the war effort and to the success of the Grand Experiment. The full suite of your abilities are necessary. I have been forced by this Koorland into committing a portion of the armies of Mars to the attack on the ork moon. No matter. It shall afford us the opportunity to acquire new materials for study, and a great number of experimental subjects for Van Auken's undertaking.'

Urquidex's logic streams shivered with misgiving at this revelation of a new experiment. His implants seized upon the statement and trapped it in data crystals embedded in his thorax for later parsing. His initial hypothesis suggested something bad.

'Perhaps my abilities might also be useful, my lord?' said Urquidex. 'I too have experience with *Veridi giganticus*.'

'You are to remain upon the Grand Experiment. Your investigations into the effects of the ork teleportation technology upon biomatter are invaluable.'

'Yes, my lord,' said Urquidex.

'We must be careful,' said the Fabricator General. 'The feuding of factions within the High Lords leaves us with no choice but to consider the ultimate divorce of our interests. There are those that suspect and work against us. Guard yourselves against them.'

A poor-quality hololith engaged, projecting a bubble of light that resolved itself into a live pict feed. In a grainy aerial view dogged by frequent cutouts and signal dispersion a woman was making her way across red sands, a breathing mask supplementing the thin Martian air.

'This individual is not as she appears,' said Kubik. 'The diagnostic covens came across erroneous data-transfer protocols. Her code signum proved to be falsified.'

'Who is she?' asked Urquidex.

'She is an operative of the Officio Assassinorum. I have been watching her for some time. Vangorich's killers are elusive, but not invisible. We observe her from a high altitude aether-drone, and she knows nothing of it.'

The woman made her way across a landscape cluttered with ancient fragments of broken machinery. The view swung around. The hive factories of Tharsis piled themselves up behind her.

'Sicarian assassin clade 950-Alpha-Xi, execute target,' commanded Kubik.

The woman stopped, alert to peril not yet visible to the magi watching the pict feed. She cast away her red robe, revealing a close-fitting combat suit and a pair of bulky pistols strapped one to each thigh. She drew them both, aimed them in opposite directions, and opened fire. The action proceeded without sound. She ran, arms outstretched and rock steady, guns blazing. Her head flicked back and forth, identifying new targets, her guns ready to follow. Urquidex was certain every shot was a kill.

'Assassins are skilled, but she is one, and we are many,' said Kubik.

An assassination clade of Sicarian ruststalkers skittered into the pict field, over twenty of them, converging on the Assassin from all sides, their long legs nimbly picking their way over the rough ground. Always seemingly on the verge of toppling over, their darting movements instead propelled them towards their target with staccato purpose, blade limbs held out to impale and slice. The Assassin upped her fire rate. Sicarians dropped, their breached pressurised armour shooting out streams of gas, spindly augmetic limbs folding in on themselves. They came closer and closer, unconcerned with their own deaths, determined only on hers. The Assassin halted, still firing, but she was surrounded and could not escape.

The Sicarians pounced on her. With a flurry of cybernetic limbs, it was done. The Assassin lay dead on the ground.

The pict view abruptly veered as the aether-drone sped away on some new task. The sky filled the image, before fizzling out.

'So end those who would profane the holy grounds of Mars,' said Kubik. His chair swivelled back and rose up high so that he could look down on the magi. 'You two have proved yourselves to me. This will be but one of a cell. We must redouble our vigilance. Spies are everywhere. We will not be thwarted so close to success.'

Urquidex struggled to control his telescopic eyes. The left

developed a tic, the lens minutely focusing and refocusing. He knew very well there were more of them. He was in regular contact with one.

'Yes, prime of primes,' Urquidex said.

He needed to speak to Yendl immediately.

NINE

The Last Wall attacks

The ork moon hung over the holy orb of Terra, a rock that threatened an imminent drop, shattering the bland grey surface of mankind's home.

But it was no longer master of the void. Space Marine ships stood off outside the range of the moon's gravity weapons, arrayed in attack formation. Seven mighty battle-barges, more than a dozen strike cruisers, scores of lesser attack ships. Behind them sheltered the huge Adeptus Mechanicus ark and factory ships, their metal bellies full of cybernetic armies ready to wreak cold vengeance upon the orks.

There was one other ship of significance in the heavens. The mighty Naval vessel *Autocephalax Eternal* stood at high anchor, treacherously doing nothing.

'Signal the *Autocephalax Eternal* again!' said Koorland. He stood upon the highest dais of the *Abhorrence*, staring at the coward Lansung's flagship through the centre of the grand oculus.

'She is still not responding, my lord Koorland,' reported one of Bohemond's bondsmen.

Koorland watched the other vessel as his own fleet flew past it.

'Anchored there, doing nothing?' said Bohemond. 'The High Admiral will answer to me himself!'

'Ignore it,' said Issachar over the fleet vox. 'There is more at play here than warfare. Some political move on the part of the High Admiral.'

'Begin the attack,' said Koorland.

In precise formation, the combined fleets of the Last Wall attacked the orks while Lansung's battleship looked on. Coming in three echelons, they speared deep into the moon's attendant flotilla, obliterating everything they came across. Ork cruisers and captured Imperial vessels burst into short-lived blossoms of fire as wide spreads of torpedoes and projectiles smashed into them. Space Marine interdiction fighters sped out from their battle-barges, driving off ork fighters that came out to meet the fleets. Adeptus Mechanicus war arks came behind, shielded by massed arrays of arcane energy projectors. On board waited the Taghmata of Mars. Cybernetic fighter drones, piloted by disembodied human brains, swarmed in close support, shooting down ork rockets and vessels that came too close.

The moon was vast, a planetoid hooked from its home and outfitted in an undeniably orkish manner. Craters had been bored out, turning them into caverns with deep black interiors studded with lights, the outer infrastructure of buried hangars poking out from them into the brilliant shine of Sol. Roughly built towers, docks and other carbuncular constructions scarred the surface. Its giant face leered at Terra, so the Space Marines saw it side on – beetling brows as large as continental shelves turned skyward, a false mountain range of a nose, a complicated mess of scaffolds and buildings a hundred kilometres long that made up the jutting lower lip. Things of greater scale existed in the galaxy, but none of them had been built by the orks.

Koorland stood at a command podium on the bridge of the *Abhorrence*. With the plan in motion, he deferred command to the individual Chapter Masters.

'Drive towards them!' ordered Bohemond. 'Smash them aside! Burn them all!'

Koorland watched with a more sober eye, adjusting his plans and counter-plans as the battle unfolded. Part of him wished he were aboard Issachar's vessel, but Bohemond had shown him great hospitality, and Koorland feared the headstrong Black Templars might stray too far forward in their desire to join with the enemy first if not supervised.

'Stay back,' said Koorland. 'We are at the extremity of the ork gravity weapons' effective range.'

Bohemond made a noise in his throat, but did not disagree openly.

'Maintain distance. Stick to the plan. Destroy the fleet. Make them come to us,' said Koorland.

The leading Space Marine ships came within lance range. Broad beams of energy striped the sky, impacting with the ork flotilla with devastating effect. Many ships detonated the moment they were hit. In response, a large part of the ork fleet surged forward.

'An ork cannot resist provocation,' said Castellan Clermont,

GUY HALEY

Bohemond's second. 'All batteries prepare to open fire! *Bona Fide* and *Ebon*, maintain protective formation.'

The moon awoke to the attack, coming alive with a frenzied sparkling as a million guns opened fire.

'This is no threat!' said Bohemond savagely. 'We alone might have bested the moon at Aspiria had dePrasse not withdrawn himself! Now the orks face the combined might of four Chapters. They shall not prevail! Attack, attack, abhor the alien!'

The leading munitions of the ork moon hurtled into the Space Marines' echelons, void shields flaring with impact flux as they struck the staggered lines of ships. More powerful weapons slashed out from tottering citadels, wavering energy beams that cut into the smaller vessels. An escort dropped out of the Fists Exemplar line, venting atmosphere from its cracked hull in white clouds.

'Stay on course! Bring the retribution of the Emperor to the fleet. Kill them all!' Spittle flew from Bohemond's ruined mouth as he spoke. Koorland could barely credit they were of the same gene line, so overpowering was the Black Templar's fervour.

'My lord,' spoke the Black Templars Techmarine, Kant. His lips were stapled together – some show of contrition, Koorland had been told, although for what the Black Templars would not reveal. His voice was a miserable metallic drone, soullessly issuing from twin vox-speakers either side of his neck. 'The ork moon exhibits a spiking of power.'

'All hands, prepare for gravity attack!' shouted Clermont.

An erratic flashing blinked in the moon's hollow craters. From pylons set about the face, squirming ribbons of energy rose, binding themselves into a thick cord. A sufficient build-up of power achieved, it snapped out like a whip, shearing through the orks' own vessels before flicking along the Excoriators arrowhead coming up below the Black Templars' line of attack. One attack cruiser took a direct hit, void shields giving out simultaneously. It imploded, the prow and stern folding up around a middle compressed to vanishingly small size. For a moment it sailed on bent double, carried forward by momentum, before exploding, buffeting the ships coming behind it with the wash of its breached reactor.

'This is a new weapon,' voxed Thane. 'I have not seen its like before.'

'Some kind of gravity lash,' said Quesadra.

'Such power!' hissed Bohemond.

'They are gathering to fire again!' warned Kant, the faintest hint of emotion creeping into his machine voice.

Once more the flickerings essayed from the towers on the surface, once more they gathered and shot out. Again the lash targeted the Excoriators fleet, grazing the fore section of the *Remembered Sin*, Issachar's flagship, as it dissipated into a kaleidoscopic spray of particles. A portion of the *Remembered Sin*'s hammerhead prow collapsed into glittering clouds of smashed metal and air. The *Remembered Sin* was twisted into a spin, as if swatted by a god.

'Issachar!' demanded Koorland. 'Status!'

'We live,' replied the Excoriator. Alarms whooped in the background. 'But we will not survive another hit like that. We must get in closer, attack the moon directly. If we can strip away its weaponry, we shall stand a chance. Push through the fleet.'

'I concur!' shouted Bohemond. 'All ships, onward! Arm cyclonic torpedoes. Target the moon.'

It irked Koorland that he did not confer with him first, but he held his silence.

'Fire control, liaise with the others,' said Koorland. 'Find a mutually acceptable firing solution. Multiple hits will give us the best results.'

'Yes, lord Chapter Master,' replied Bohemond's bondsmen.

The *Abhorrence*'s engines opened up, pushing it with indomitable power towards the moon.

The sky around Terra was thick with debris. Shattered orbital fortresses and defence platforms floated in shoals of wreckage, making sailing hazardous for both sides. Ork fighters, keen to engage with the approaching ships, impacted with them in flashes of boiling fire. The Space Marine pilots, more cautious, better skilled, were taxed to the limit streaking through the metal-choked vacuum. The bigger ships could not avoid the debris, and all across the Last Wall void shields flashed and curled with impact flux.

'Gravity lash arming,' droned Kant.

'Firing solution agreed, all fleets report readiness.' The bondsmen manning the gunnery station looked to Koorland.

A number of impact points flashed up on the hololith of the ork moon. Koorland nodded.

'All ships, open fire,' he ordered.

Cyclonic torpedoes, each larger than a space fighter, slipped free of the launch tubes of twenty battle-barges and strike cruisers. Their engines flared, and they powered towards the moon with building speed, passing the emissions of the gravity lash coming the other way.

Now they were closer, the lash struck with redoubled violence. The tip of it took the battle-barge of one of the Black Templars' subsidiary crusades in the centre. The lash writhed and coiled about it like a python, collapsing the ship's midsection so comprehensively that the remains of the prow and stern drifted free of each other. The stern detonated with the sunburst of reactor death, engulfing its escort vessels in nuclear fire. The lash had not done: it twitched through the crusade's ships, smashing two more of them into nothing before finally dissipating. When it shut off, a single vessel remained, heavily damaged. It was targeted by a flight of ork destroyers. Fire sped between the crippled Imperial ship and its predators, but there could be only one outcome. The ship disappeared, replaced by a perfect circle of brilliant light that winked out as quickly as it bloomed.

Bohemond roared at the oculus, slamming his fist into his palm. 'They will pay all the more dearly for that!' he yelled. 'Prepare to fire a second volley of torpedoes.'

The first launch had reached the moon, slamming all over the surface. Explosions lit up tits face with domes of fire and light. The moon shook under the impact. Tall plumes of ejecta reared up, gnarled fingers reaching for the Space Marine ships.

'Ready to fire again!' reported gunnery command.

'Hold!' ordered Koorland as Bohemond raised his hand. 'Wait for the others.'

'Koorland,' said Bohemond.

'Wait!' commanded the Imperial Fist. 'We are most effective working in concert. You will wait!'

Shorter-ranged grav-weapons began their assault on the fleet. Clouds of energy bubbles projected at the ships crushed all those they touched. Long-ranged reverse tractor beams tore pieces from hulls or pushed vessels off course. For all the havoc wreaked on the moon's surface, there were hundreds of thousands of weapons still, of all types, unleashing their full power on the approaching vessels. Void shields throbbed, and across the fleets they failed with oily pyrotechnic displays. Battle-barges shook under the barrage. Several of the smaller vessels were destroyed.

By now the fleets were close to the moon, deep in the debris field. Here were thousands of captured Imperial vessels, many undergoing crude refits. The broadsides of the capital ships boomed constantly, blasting ork craft and pirated Imperial ships to pieces. Destroyers duelled with fast ork attack craft, and everywhere tracers of anti-interdiction fire streaked the sky.

Icons flashed across Koorland's station. Vox-confirmation came in from the rest of the fleet.

'Now. Now open fire, High Marshal,' said Koorland.

'Do as he commands, open fire!' roared Bohemond, but his men had already responded.

More torpedoes raced towards the moon, pounding into the surface. The weight of fire issuing from the moon lessened.

'Brother Kant, is the gravity lash disabled?'

'Negative,' said Kant. 'They are charging to fire again.'

'My lords! We have reports of multiple boarders across the fleets,' reported the vox-master. 'Teleport attack.'

'They will have taken these craft the same way. They will not find us so easy to overpower,' said Bohemond. 'Seal the bulkheads! Weapons free. Activate corridor defences.'

'It is done, my lord.'

Koorland pressed his knuckles into his command station. 'Bring the fleet around, get us between Terra and the face. The pylons have to be brought down.'

'Too late!' shouted Kant.

The gravity lash arced directly towards the *Abhorrence*. The bondsman at the helm shouted, 'Evasive action!' and the ship plunged as quickly as it was able. The ribbon of gravitic energy raced over the command tower as it slipped down, shearing into the engine stacks of the battle-barge as they presented themselves.

The ship lurched madly as the gravity wave perturbed its course, throwing men everywhere, an effect that worsened enormously when the beam cut into the stern. Koorland slammed against his command post and fell over it, the effects of the ork weapon making a mockery of the *Abhorrence*'s grav-plating. He fell down a deck that was suddenly vertical, skidding along the metal towards the back of the ship. Somehow, he got his feet under him and activated his maglocks. He lurched upright painfully, standing perpendicularly to the upended gravity. Men flew past him, dragged towards the artificial gravity well of the lash.

The ship rolled violently to port. Through the oculus, Koorland saw the *Bona Fide* burning engines hard to clear the stricken vessel's path. With a further mighty wrench to portside, the beam shut off. Gravity returned suddenly to the correct vector. Bondsmen slid down the back wall. Unsecured articles fell from the ceiling. Alarms blared, tocsins sang. The lights had gone out, replaced by the murky red of emergency lumens. Men groaned in pain. A dozen of them did not get up, but lay still.

Throughout it all, Kant had remained stoically anchored in place by his master augur array. 'We have lost our port engine assembly, my liege. There is heavy damage across all decks in the aft section. Several of our tower superstructures are no more. Multiple casualties among our bondsmen and servitors.'

Bohemond picked himself up from the floor. Bondsmen medicae teams hurried in to help their stricken comrades.

'Get us back on heading. Continue attack run.'

'Gravity weapon charging again.'

'My lords!' called a bondsman at the auspex centre. 'My lords, we have the energy signature of a large fleet approaching from Terra's nightside.'

'It cannot be the Imperial Navy. The *Autocephalax Eternal* stands off, and there are no other Naval vessels in the system,' said Bohemond.

'There was no warning of orks on the far side of the throne-world,' said Koorland.

'Gravity weapon is close to full charge,' warned Kant.

'Brace!' shouted Clermont. The lightning discharge built, and Koorland prepared for the worst.

The attack never came. The face side of the ork moon appeared to change shape, redrawn by a swift painter working in blinding light. The oculus dimmed itself at the sudden fire, and the Space Marines saw the moon's face deformed by a dozen atomic blasts.

From out of the maelstrom a fresh fleet came sailing, jet-black silhouettes set against the destruction they had unleashed.

Adeptus Astartes vessels.

A powerful, sonorous voice burst over the vox.

'This is Chapter Master Malfons. The Iron Knights respond to the call of the Last Wall. We apologise for our tardiness, but we are here. The sons of Dorn stand together. Awaiting orders.'

'The gravity lash is disabled,' said Kant. 'Auspex indicates eighty per cent of all ork surface weaponry non-functional.'

'Malfons!' shouted Bohemond. 'Well met, brother!'

'Continue attack run,' ordered Koorland. 'All fleets converge. Establish blockade pattern. Iron Knights, support the Fists Exemplar.'

'Understood and confirmed, Chapter Master Koorland. And Koorland?'

'Yes, brother?'

'You have our regret at your loss. Moving in to support the Fists Exemplar now.'

All around the moon, the night of the void turned to mottled day as the Space Marines broke off their charge to the moon, and dealt death to the remaining ork fleet. Caught within expertly intersected fields of fire, the ork vessels and captured Imperial mercantile ships were torn to pieces.

'Now the real work begins. What will you do, brother?' said Bohemond with an appraising look. 'Join the fray, or remain here? You are the last of the Imperial Fists. Perhaps you should not risk yourself.'

'Who will lead the attack? You?'

'If you so command, then I will gladly lead,' said Bohemond.

Koorland examined Bohemond's scarred face, but could not read the fragment of expression displayed there.

'All fleets of the Last Wall, prepare to board the moon,' Koorland ordered. 'Adeptus Mechanicus arks, the way is clear for you to move in and begin your deployment.' Koorland turned to Bohemond. 'I will lead an attack party myself.'

Bohemond gave him a wild look. 'In that case, brother, I have a gift for you.'

The ork bombardment had ceased, and now the halls of the *Abhorrence* resounded with the activity of men. As bondsmen and the servants of the Black Templars' forge ran towards the vessel's damaged sections, squads of Space Marines jogged towards their drop-halls and the embarkation deck.

In Bohemond's personal arming chambers, silence held sway. The cowled bondsmen still went about their business as if nothing had occurred, checking Bohemond's collection of weapons for upset and damage, and setting right that which had been disturbed. Bohemond led Koorland through his spartan dayroom, through a small weapons workshop, an ammunition store and thence into his innermost sanctum, an octagonal room lined floor to ceiling with weaponry. Most of it was of fine Imperial make, adorned with emblems of the shield and the Templar cross, honour chains and shackles coiled carefully onto pegs beneath each mount. Intermingled were a number of weapons of alien make, of all types from the obvious to the obscure of purpose.

'You are surprised?' said Bohemond, when he caught Koorland examining the xenos devices. 'These are my trophies, many taken from worthy opponents, unclean though they were... But there would be no honour in employing the weapons of the alien against the alien. What I have for you is of far nobler origin.' He pointed to an alcove where waited a large object covered with a white silk shroud, black Templar crosses repeated hundreds of times over it in an interlocking pattern. Bohemond nodded at one of his arming bondsmen. The man came forward and tugged the shroud free.

Underneath was a suit of Terminator armour, painted in the bold yellow of the Imperial Fists.

'This suit is one of the very first of the Indomitus armours manufactured,' said Bohemond, indicating the familiar planed helm and heavy-gauge chest plating. 'Its name is *Fidus Bellator*, and it was fashioned in the closing years of the great Heresy war.' He looked at Koorland. 'I doubted you, Koorland. I cannot deny it. I have yet to be convinced you are suitable to lead the assembled might of the Last Wall. Yet you have proved yourself in other ways. You are confident, sure of purpose, tactically astute. You are worthy of the rank of Chapter Master, and so I may yet change my mind. In recognition, and in friendship, I give this to you.'

'I do not know what to say, High Marshal,' said Koorland wonderingly. Much of his Chapter's supplies and materiel had been destroyed around Ardamantua, though there would of course be armour and weapons still aboard their great star fortress of the *Phalanx* and in their barracks on Terra. But were there any Terminator suits left? He doubted it. They were all lost, along with the First Company.

'Then say nothing,' said Bohemond. 'The armour is not dishonoured, for *Fidus Bellator* has borne these colours before. Once it resided in the armouriums of the *Phalanx*. If it makes it easier to accept, let us agree that I do nothing more than return it home.'

'You do me a great honour. I cannot repay you.'

'I do,' agreed Bohemond. 'And you can repay me. Repay me with glory, Chapter Master. Avenge your brothers.'

TEN

The gate

An electric buzzing supplanted Koorland's senses as his substance was projected through the warp. His body diffused, becoming a tingling sensation and little else. Thought fled as his consciousness momentarily disconnected from reality, but it did not cease – rather his sense of self became something else, a raw awareness without thought, a thing of feeling. Rationality was inconceivable. Time was irrelevant. There was only being, nothing else.

A wall of pain interrupted his contemplations. His body passed out of the warp, his wargear and flesh rearranging themselves into solid forms. A blaze of light and rush of vapour, and he was striding forward, gun raised, into a roughly hewn chamber cluttered with ramshackle machinery and orks. A subsidiary power nexus for the surface energy weapons, its destruction would knock out several dozen energy cannons, or so their Adeptus Mechanicus allies had informed them.

The xenos recovered quickly from their surprise at

Koorland appearing in their midst, abandoning the tasks they were about at the machines, and launched themselves at the Space Marine with a ferocious roaring. Their weapons rebounded from his Terminator armour without effect. Koorland gunned them down with his storm bolter, blasting them into bouncing pieces. Ork slave creatures squealed and ran from him. Rushing air behind him signalled other successful teleports. The sensorium of his borrowed suit pinged into life, triangulating his location, linking up with the auspex suites of his ad hoc squad.

'Teleport successful. Target achieved. Strike Team Slaughter, respond,' he voxed. He could not turn easily in the massive armoured suit, not without presenting his back to the doorway.

'Moscht here,' spoke a voice into his helm. The Space Marines sounded off, their squad icons and vital signs flicking into life upon Koorland's helm display.

'Ulferic here.'

'Donafen here.'

'Arbalt here.'

'Holde here.'

Two Black Templars, a brother of the Fists Exemplar, an Excoriator, and an Iron Knight made up his small command.

'Zero casualties,' said Koorland.

'Praise be,' said Ulferic and Arbalt.

Koorland ignored their odd expression of piety. 'Thus far, our Adeptus Mechanicus allies have been proven correct. According to their information, the primary target is this way – power generators for the ork gravity weapons. Let us ensure they never fire again. Move out and engage.'

Koorland went first, the others close behind. The combat chatter of other Terminator squads crackled in his ears.

Three hundred Terminators worked their way through the tunnels. The moon shook with impacts from the surface, shortly joined by the detonation of demolition charges nearer to hand. Data-screed and vox-reports kept Koorland abreast of the battle, so much information it took the superior mind of a Space Marine to comprehend.

'Target Gamma destroyed.'

'Report heavy fire, sector nineteen forty-three.'

'Target Zeta damaged and on fire. Proceeding to secondary objectives.'

Koorland's squad stamped through corridors carved from grey stone, primitive deck plating buckling under the weight of their armour. Squads of orks burst from doorways, weapons blazing. Their large-calibre bullets ricocheted from the thick plates of the Terminator suits in showers of hot sparks. Return fire cut them down. As they passed each rathole and stinking entrance, Holde of the Iron Knights poked the nozzle of his heavy flamer down it and sent a jet of shrieking promethium inside. Burning ork slave creatures ran out, screaming. Soon the twisting corridors were choked with smoke, and the Space Marines switched to artificially enhanced views of their environs.

They approached their target. The corridor widened into a cavern, floored erratically with platforms of poorly cut metal. Rough doors as numerous as maggot holes in a corpse riddled the chamber sides. A four-storey-tall machine buzzed and crackled in the middle of the cavern, topped by a rotating arrangement of three glass balls as big as light tanks whose innards writhed with peculiar energies.

'Our primary target is ahead of us,' voxed Koorland. 'Destroy it.'

'First, a little bladeplay,' said Arbalt, pointing across the uneven cavern floor.

From an entrance on the far side, hundreds of orks pelted into the room, howling guttural xenos war cries, each one desperate to be the first to kill. Gunfire hammered down at the Space Marines from the tiered galleries ranged up the walls.

Koorland raised his gun and his power sword in salute. 'For the Emperor,' he said.

The Terminators opened fire.

In her dreams, Haas laboured. An eternity had passed since her arrival, and whether it was days or aeons long, she could not tell. There was no marker to judge by, no day-night cycle. It was never dark and it was never truly light. Food and water came rarely and erratically. The orks were capricious in everything, sticking to no schedule or plan. They let the prisoners sleep at random times for periods that could have been minutes or hours. Without a chronopiece, there was no way of knowing.

During their 'day', she and the longshanks were shackled together and marched a short distance from their cell to the lift platforms leading to the giant hollow in the heart of the moon. There they were whipped and beaten and forced to move supplies under conditions of erratic gravity. They worked in the shadow of the orks' crackling gate, a spasming vortex of green fire whose flarings spat out raw materials, goods, food and always more and more orks. The noise from it was terrifying, a constant thunder that boomed deafeningly loud with every fresh transit.

It was there that Haas was dragged to work, and there she returned during her brief nightmares.

The ork gate shimmered over her head, bathing the sandy floor of the transit cave in painful light. An ork was coming, the one they called One Tooth, for the single ivory fang jutting over his lip. She kept her head down, not wanting to be noticed. But One Tooth was coming for her, growing to incredible dream-size.

'Too little, too runty,' it said. Tiny slave things scuttled around its feet, repeating its words mockingly. 'Far too weak! To the meat room, take it to the meat room!'

A huge hand, horny with callouses lined with old blood, reached down for her.

She came awake screaming when it touched her.

'Shhh!' said Marast, touching his lips with a single long finger. 'Quiet! Something's happening.'

All around the dim cell the longshanks were stirring, unfolding spindly limbs from their uncomfortable sleeping positions and looking towards the door.

'What?' said Haas. Gunfire and shouting came from outside, down on the prison cavern floor.

An explosion rocked the room, followed by a storm of gunfire.

'What's going on?' shouted Marast. The other slaves screamed at the noise.

'The orks!' said Haas. 'They're being attacked!' She was up on her feet, adrenaline keeping her exhaustion at bay. She crept towards the door. The light of weapons discharge strobed through the viewing slit. She stood on tiptoes to look through.

'Get her away from there!' hissed Huringer.

'What's happening?' asked Marast.

'Can't see. Wait...' Haas shrieked and threw herself backwards as a pair of glaring red eyes appeared at the slit.

The ork rumbled aggressively in its alien tongue. Keys jangled, and it flung the door open.

The ork swaggered in, kicking the longshanks aside with bone-crushing force. Battle noise flooded the room. The ork slaver ignored it, his head swinging back and forward, nose snuffling. Haas scrambled back, until her back was against the wall by the door. The ork caught sight of her and pointed, gabbling in its uncouth language. A blind, stupid hatred of such intensity shone in its eyes that Haas was pinned by its gaze, unable to move.

It said something and smiled evilly. As it had in her dream, it reached massive hands out for her.

A series of bangs resounded round the room. The ork's chest blew out messily, showering Haas with viscera. She covered her face instinctively. A final shot rang out, bursting its head, and its huge corpse toppled towards her. Haas scrambled aside to see a giant warrior in black-and-white armour shove itself into the cell, bringing part of the doorway down. It was some kind of Space Marine, garbed in armour Haas had never seen: tall, high-backed, the helmet roughly square and formed of brutal angular plates, arms protected by massive shoulder guards. A second stood in the door, watching his comrade's back.

'Thank the Emperor! We are saved, saved!' shouted Marast. He flung his lanky body at the feet of the Space Marine, clutching gratefully at the feet of their saviours. The longshanks wept, disbelieving of their salvation.

The Space Marine nudged Marast away with its enormous boot.

'Non-standard human phenotype identified. Loathe the mutant. Terminate.'

Haas curled up and clapped her hands over her ears as the Space Marines opened fire with their terrible weapons. The longshanks did not even have time to express their surprise before their fragile bodies were pulped by mass-reactive shells. The gunfire went on forever, the individual reports merging into one rolling booming. When it stopped, Haas was amazed to find she still lived. Her hands shook as she took them from her ears. The longshanks had been obliterated, reduced to a gory slick that dripped from the walls.

Her ears hurt agonisingly and she cried out. The Space Marine swung its blocky helmet in her direction, pointing its bolter at her. She screamed again, and the Space Marine moved his bolter away from her. When he spoke to her it was muffled, as if her ears were stuffed with fabric.

'Human survivor located. You, come with us.' The warrior pointed a massive articulated finger at her, the segments sparking with a power field. 'The Emperor protects.'

Hundreds of dead orks lay in piles around the cave, by the burning machine, on the floor, on the walkways, in cell doors. A handful more of the Space Marines in the massive armour stood at the far end, weapons smoking. Their liveries were all different. Haas only recognised the bright yellow of an Imperial Fist. From the rear of the cavern Space Marines in more familiar armour were flooding in, dozens

of them, drawn from the same Chapters as those in the oversized wargear.

One of her rescuers walked away on another errand, the high, hunched back of his armour swaying, the walkway rocking dangerously under his weight. The other shepherded her down rickety stairs to the cavern floor, bringing her together with a few bewildered humans like herself. They were guided to where the Imperial Fist stood, directing the incoming warriors into defensive positions.

'Chapter Master Koorland, human survivors,' said her rescuer. The chamber shook with a titanic impact somewhere high above. Grit pattered down from the roof.

The Imperial Fist, Koorland, finished giving his orders to warriors in bare metal armour discoloured by heat, and others in battered gear annotated with careful script.

'State your names,' said Koorland to the survivors. 'Be quick. If you have anything worthwhile to tell us of the ork moon, reveal it now. We cannot tarry.'

Haas began to speak. A tracked ammunition train came clanking into the chamber, drowning out her voice. The larger warriors stumped over to it, moving slowly but with purpose. Servitors opened hoppers in the train's sides and began rearming weapons, while others with specialised tools for limbs ran diagnostic checks on the Space Marines' armour and effected minor repairs. Others in the giant battlesuits were arriving from elsewhere, and these were also attended to. The noise in the chamber was deafening, warriors shouting, heavy footsteps booming off uneven deck plating. The other rescued men and women said nothing, other than babbling thanks and praise. The Imperial Fist turned from them, as if he had never expected to receive anything of use from them.

Haas tried again.

'Your men! They killed the longshanks,' she shouted.

The Chapter Master turned back.

'What?' His voice was hard and inhuman from his vox-grille, the bright yellow helm unreadable. Haas was terrified, but her instinct for justice was strong.

'Others. I was imprisoned with them. They helped keep me safe, and your men killed them.'

'You are?'

'Arbitrator Galatea Haas, Imperial Palace 149th Administrative District, General Oversight Division. I survived the Proletarian Crusade.'

'Is this true, Arbalt?' Koorland asked of Haas' rescuer.

'The female was domiciled with a number of aberrants,' said Arbalt, his contempt plainly audible through the distortions of his vox-grille. 'Non-standard humanoid phenotype. They did not deserve clemency.'

'They told me that they were permitted abhumans. Longshanks,' said Haas.

'Longshanks? That kind are not mutants,' said Koorland. 'Arbalt, Ulferic. No human is to be harmed, no matter their type, not before you report to me.'

'As you wish, Chapter Master,' said Arbalt emotionlessly.

'Convey this information to all your fellows,' he said angrily. 'While you are under my command I will not countenance the needless slaying of innocents.'

Arbalt gave an awkward bow, his movements restricted by his suit. 'My lord Chapter Master.'

'You may go,' said Koorland to the humans.

'There is more,' said Haas. 'The orks. They have a... a device, not far from here. A gate.'

Koorland looked down at her. His helmet's muzzle and odd faceted panels made him look like an animal made of metal. 'A gate?'

'Some kind of teleportation device,' said Haas. 'Troops and weapons come through it all the time.'

Koorland motioned for a Space Marine wearing rust-red armour, a bulky servo-arm folded on top of his pack. 'Send word to the Adeptus Mechanicus. We have intelligence of interest.'

'Immediately, Chapter Master Koorland.' The Space Marine hurried away.

Koorland called another to him. 'Fetch this woman food and water. Now.' Only then did he give his full attention to Haas. He tilted forward a little and projected a rough holo-lith from a device integrated into his suit.

'This is a three-dimensional representation of the immediate surroundings,' he said. 'Show me where this "gate" is...'

ELEVEN

Servant of the Beast

The moon ceased shuddering. The fleet's efforts to strip the weaponry from the surface were concluded, but throughout the interior Space Marines fought desperate close battles against hordes of green monsters, protecting Adeptus Mechanicus salvage teams and xenologists while they stripped whole caverns of machinery. The orks, though contained, did not diminish in number.

The woman Haas had been correct. Through a grainy pict image relayed from the eyes of a servo-skull probe to a portable augur station, Koorland, Bohemond and Thane saw the orkish gate in operation. The skull looked down from a ledge high overhead. The angle was odd, the picture a striated, brown monochrome, but the poor quality of the image could not disguise the scale of what they witnessed. The orks had carved a chamber four kilometres across to house it. Bizarre machines crowded the walls, crackling with potent energies. Within the circle of the machines, piles of crates, scrap, lesser machines and weapons occupied

the flat, gravelly floor. Fat cables snaked away through the materiel crowding the chamber, plugging the gate into the machines.

The gate itself was made up of three metal horns, as tall as Titans, curving up from a crudely made platform suspended some metres above the cavern floor. Steel hawsers, chains and ungainly clamps held them in place. They wobbled even so, perturbed by the energies they contained. Constant, dancing light jumped at the centre. Every few minutes, the light shone brighter, almost whiting out the pict, and yet another mob of thick-shouldered, tusked greenskins stomped out onto the platform, hefting their weapons, eager to fight.

'The moons. They are not simple spacecraft as we assumed,' said Koorland. 'They are bridgeheads. It is no wonder the planets attacked have been so easily overwhelmed.'

'Where have they learned technology of this power?' said Bohemond. 'With each encounter we uncover further disquieting information. Is there no limit to their ingenuity?'

'We have not seen this before,' said Thane. 'What has changed?'

'Fascinating,' said Kant. 'Their mastery of the gravitic sciences must be connected with this. There is potential here. It is said the eldar possess something similar, a sub-spatial network that enables communication between their scattered worlds.'

'Such an ability in the hands of the orks is an unwelcome proposition,' said Koorland. 'This must be what Kubik was so keen to secure.'

'I concur with his desire,' said Kant. 'The orks are epidemic.

These machines can only make that situation worse. This is surely the reason for the Beast's success. We must capture it, study it. Then we might counter it.'

They watched as another rabble of orks marched out of the flashing tunnel of light.

'While they keep their tunnel open, we cannot defeat them,' said Thane. 'Terra will become an eternal battleground. The orks will replenish their numbers as ours dwindle. The gate must close, the moon must fall.'

'It can be done,' said Bohemond. 'If that sybaritic coward Lansung can best one, then it should be a small matter for us.'

'The agreement with Mars was that the moon must be taken,' said Kant. 'This gate is the greatest prize of all.'

'No,' said Koorland. 'The gate must be destroyed.'

'We shall see to it,' said Bohemond.

Kant agreed dolefully. 'It saddens me, but I can only concur. Maybe some knowledge might be gleaned from the wreckage.'

'I suggest massed Terminator assault,' said Bohemond. 'Only by meeting them with the First Companies and Sword Brethren of our orders can we hope to prevail. Once we attack the gate, the orks will be stirred to heights of fury. We might fight our way there, but escape? Teleportation will be the only viable means of extraction.'

'Thane?' asked Koorland.

'There are multiple plans that would result in the destruction of the gate, but I cannot conceive of another that would not result in an unacceptable toll of gene-seed and life. Teleportation through so much mass and shielding as the moon possesses can only be realistically achieved by those in Terminator plate. We would lose many power-armoured brothers. Bohemond's suggestion has great merit.'

'What is your proposition, High Marshal?' said Koorland. 'Form a cordon, fight our way in?'

'From multiple directions,' said Bohemond. He called up a wireframe diagrammatic of the moon, displacing the pict feed from their augur screen. Much of the ork satellite had been mapped by deep auspex, but there were large areas shaded in red, lacking detail. 'Our Chapters hold large parts of the moon. The ork reinforcements must be using these tunnels here to come to their fellows' aid direct from the gate.' He indicated three straight tunnels, wide as highways, that led from the gate chamber to the surface, where they exited from the apertures of the moon's giant ork face. Dozens of lesser ways threaded from them, riddling the crust and deeper interior.

'We must divert their attention,' said Thane. 'These orks are strange, and apt to use many unusual technologies, but look at them. Projected from the other side of the galaxy, they come out roaring and snorting, hungry for war. Whatever new tricks these beasts have mastered, they remain orks.'

'Orks cannot resist a direct challenge,' said Bohemond. 'Provoke them, and we may direct their fury as we might. Let us send word to the fleet and land our armoured vehicles. Deploy them in the tunnels – that is a lure no ork could resist. They will die before the guns of our tanks while we attack from the rear.'

* * *

A taskforce-wide vox-blurt signalled the beginning of the attack. Across the main triple highway into the core the massed tanks of five Chapters advanced. In the subsidiary tunnels to the sides, hundreds of Space Marines fanned out to stop any orks who might choose an alternative route around the advancing Land Raiders, Razorbacks and Predators. The moon rumbled with new detonations as vital passageways were brought down, blocked with millions of tons of rock and metal. At the peripheries of the territories held by the Chapters, Space Marines prepared for the moment the orkish reinforcements would be cut off. Thereafter they were to drive forward, trapping the remaining greenskins.

There would be slaughter, Koorland was sure, but the cost in gene-forged blood would be high.

The Terminators worked their way into position around the gate as the orks took the bait, advancing up the main tunnels where they hurled themselves at the advancing Space Marine tanks. The armour worked its way forward purposefully, slowly, the tunnel resonating with the reports of their weapons and the howling of orks.

Koorland fought alongside Thane and his bodyguard of Terminators. Through a labyrinth they proceeded, slaughtering orks wherever they found them. The corridors rarely ran straight, and where battle was met it was a vicious, close-quarters affair. Koorland's freshly painted armour was soon a mess of nicks and scratches, the bright yellow stained dark red. His sword was caked from tip to pommel in blood baked black by its power field.

'This feels good,' grunted Thane, smashing an ork's head

deep into its shoulders with his power maul. 'On Eidolica, we kept them back as long as we could, slaying them with our guns. Tactically proper, but where vengeance is involved, I prefer to see my enemy's face close.' He let out a shout as he smashed another ork down. Koorland cut the hands from his own opponent with a single well-placed blow. The ork roared its anger and battered at him with bloody wrists. Koorland spared a single round from his storm bolter to end it.

'Close-quarter melee conserves our ammunition,' said Thane at the sound of the gun. 'We are going to need it.'

They rounded a corner. The corridor opened up onto the floor of the gate chamber. Thousands of orks were pouring from the flaring mechanism.

'There are so many. It is as Eidolica was,' said Thane.

'So it was on Ardamantua also,' said Koorland. 'An endless tide. Let us stop it up. Time to announce ourselves!'

Thane strode into the chamber, selected a tall crackling machine for his ire, and smashed its casing with his power maul. Sheet metal caved in, exposing the flashing innards. Another blow arrested its processes explosively. Fire belched from the array of pipes on the top, followed by a greasy cough of smoke.

'Destroy the machines! Destroy them all!' roared Thane.

'Interrupt the power supply,' said Koorland. 'Close the gate.'

Five more machines died before the orks noticed their attackers. Piggish, ugly faces turned at the sound of the destruction. Without breaking stride, a portion of the orks streaming from the gate up the tunnels changed direction, and charged at the new threat.

'Now is the proper time for the expenditure of ammunition,' shouted Thane. 'First Company, fire!'

Forty of Thane's Terminators formed a bowed line centred on him, while the others fanned out and destroyed the machines. Their guns spoke with one booming voice. Storm bolters on full automatic blazed a streaking hail of fiery darts. Assault cannons spun up to firing speed, spitting out a torrent of bullets. Where bolts met orkish flesh, they penetrated and exploded. Orks staggered on with horrendous injuries. Many required two or three further shots to down. Where they encountered the furious sweep of the assault cannons, they were cut in half. The orks stumbled and fell, or were blown backwards in bloody chunks. Stacks of supply crates were shredded. Munitions within them detonated. Shoulder-launched cyclone missiles exploded in tight clusters, tearing red holes in the ork hordes. The enemy tumbled over the corpses of their fellows, piled high by their own momentum, a line of ruined flesh at the edge of the Space Marines' range. Still they came.

All over the cavern, explosions roared upward as other Terminator groups entered the hall and set to work. Koorland headed implacably towards the nearest of the gate horns. He smashed down an ork that had made its way through the torrent of fire. An electric fizzling crackled across the chamber as a tall, horizontal wheel covered in bronze balls came off its mountings. Green lightning jagged out into walls, floor and machinery. Another huge boom, and another. Gouts of fire rolled upward.

'Company, change ranks!' yelled Thane. His first line, their ammunition exhausted, stepped back, smoothly changing places with another line that stepped forward, storm bolters already chattering. There was no interruption to the wall of death the Fists Exemplar dealt out.

Koorland and his entourage were beyond the edge of the firing line, and the orks came more thickly. They brought them down, smashing their way towards the horn. Koorland cut the cables running along the floor. Fires blazed everywhere, tinged with green, choking black smoke billowing from them, moving strangely in the erratic artificial gravity of the gate room. The gate stuttered, its light and its buzzing interrupted. Orks passing through during this intermission were torn in half.

'Press on, press on!' roared Koorland. The flow of orks lessened. The gate blinked off again, longer this time. Koorland emptied his magazine into an important-looking machine, blasting it to bits.

The gate went out. The orks roared as one. All around the chamber they were facing lines of Space Marine Terminators. At measured pace, the Space Marine lines converged, trapping the orks between them. The sons of Dorn suffered their losses, but for every champion of humanity that fell, twenty orks died. The orks flooding up the tunnel towards the tank line milled about, unsure which enemy to engage. They surged back and forth, before finally switching direction and running towards the Terminators.

At Thane's position the guns of the second line clicked empty. No third line existed to replace them. The orks clambered over their heaped dead, and charged into the Space Marine ranks.

A cacophony of weapons hitting thick battleplate

announced the meeting of orks and Space Marines, followed by the banging of matter annihilated by disruption fields as the Adeptus Astartes swung their power fists.

'Onward, to the gate horn!' ordered Koorland. Orks pulled at his arms, thick green fingers slipping from his gory armour. He shook them off. The horn towered over him. He pulled out the melta bomb maglocked to his thigh, twisted the flask handle, and slapped it into place. Two more Terminators followed, attaching their own bombs. Across the smoking, empty platform, Koorland saw Bohemond and Issachar's warriors doing the same, Malfons himself attaching his bomb to the third horn.

'Charges placed,' voxed the lord of the Iron Knights.

'Withdraw,' voxed Koorland. 'Prepare for extraction. Our work here is over for today. Initiate teleport countdown.'

On his chronometer, five minutes flashed up, and began to tick down.

'Terminator groups, withdraw to predesignated teleport coordinates.'

All around the chamber, the Terminators backed away, always facing the enemy. The orks were greatly reduced in number, but thousands remained, and their fury only grew as their ranks were further thinned.

At three minutes, ten seconds until teleport the gate flared again. Through the flickering light stepped the largest ork Koorland had ever seen. Not even the warlords of the great tribal migrations he had fought against compared with it. It was taller than a Space Marine Dreadnought, an axe as big as a Rhino's side in its hand. Red eyes glowed with feral intelligence above a row of close-packed teeth as long as sabres. Upon its head was a thick helmet, adorned with a spread of horns as long as power swords. Around it were thirty or so other orks, smaller than their leader but every one a terrible warrior in its own right.

The giant ork shouted out an incomprehensible stream of xenos words, and the orks fighting the Space Marines began to rally themselves, pulling back into better order, firing their guns at the Terminators.

'What by the Emperor is that thing?' voxed Malfons. 'Is it the Beast itself?'

'Whatever it is, it is a worthy foe,' said Bohemond.

The orks redoubled their attack as their master stepped off the gateway platform. Its monstrous bodyguard swaggered after it, wargear and weaponry uniform only in their brutality. As they stepped down, more orks were revealed behind. Some bore banner poles of iron fists clutching spanner icons. All of them wore harnesses and aprons stuffed full of tools, and their weapons were bizarre combinations of heavy axes and wrenches. These ran across the platform, jumping off the sides. They headed for the wrecked machines, dozens of slave assistants rushing after them. The leader beast roared and gesticulated, pointing to the worst damage. Now some of the orks retreated, forming a cordon, blocking the Terminators' way to the specialists. Behind a line of warriors twenty deep, the mechanicians set to work. The rest of the orks roared and charged. The two lines of Space Marines met, and smoothly reformed into a circle.

'They are repairing the machines,' said Malfons.

'Ignore them!' ordered Koorland. 'They have not seen the

melta charges. When they do, they will not have time to disarm them. Teleport in two minutes, twenty seconds. We must prevail until then!' Koorland swept his power sword across the front rank of orks, cutting several in two with one swipe. The rest surged on over the toppling bodies of their friends, driven on by the crowd behind and their own insatiable battle lust.

'Hold them back! Hold them back!' roared Koorland.

Two minutes to teleport.

The circle of Space Marines shrank. For all the thickness of their armour, they were heavily outnumbered.

The great beast lofted its axe, and brought it down with a powerful swing to point at Koorland. Shouting more orders, it bore down on the last of the Imperial Fists with a plodding charge, head down, its bodyguard forming an arrowhead behind it.

Koorland slew his last opponent, and prepared to meet it.

Those Space Marines still possessing ammunition opened fire. For a few vital seconds mass-reactives shattered thick armour plates, blew divots of green flesh from massive muscles, then the ork charge hit home. The orks towered over the Space Marine elite, and knocked them staggering. Chainaxes rose and fell, hacking through reinforced ada- mantium and ceramite by dint of raw orkish strength. Boxy power klaw blades squealed through hardened metal, snip- ping off heads and limbs. The Space Marines fought back, smashing the orks with their power fists, caving in their ribs and crushing their faces into bloody mist.

The leader came at Koorland, and the Imperial Fist had the fight of his life on his hands.

Thirty seconds to teleport.

The ork was twice Koorland's height, broader than a battle tank. Koorland sidestepped its lowered head, but was caught upon the thing's shoulder and sent stumbling backwards. His armour's gyroscopic stabilisation systems protested as they fought to keep him upright. The ork recovered swiftly, swinging its massive axe out and across at Koorland's chest height. It hit his plastron, the impact of the blow shaking him inside his armour. The eagle upon his chest was wrecked, the metal detail pressed and smashed into itself as if it had been crafted from soft lead. The ork reared up, raising its axe before Koorland could react. The weapon hurtled down, fast as a comet. Koorland pivoted awkwardly, pushing the mobility of his armour to its limit to raise his sword in an overhead parry.

His weapon met the cruel head of the axe with a titanic *boom*. The axe head exploded into spinning, white-hot shrapnel. The force of the blow was such that Koorland was driven to his knee. When he lumbered back upright, he found his own blade was a blackened shard. He had no time to order his armour to disconnect the power feed and discard it. The beast was on him again, its skin studded with the smoking remains of its axe.

Twenty seconds to teleport.

The ork reached down, grabbing both of Koorland's arms in its gargantuan fists. It lifted him up, armour and all, pulling his arms apart. Koorland's armour sang a litany of alarms. Red flashed all over his helm display. Metal groaned, and hot pain stabbed into his wrists, elbows and shoulders as the joints began to part.

The cavern filled with golden light as the melta bombs went off in stepped detonations, micro-fusion devices slagging wide rings of the left gate horn. Sectioned into pieces, the device slid apart, spraying gobbets of molten metal into the orks around the teleport gate. Then the second fell, and the third, tearing metal shrieking, severed power lines lashing back and forth with frantic energies.

The pressure slackened as the leader ork looked back at the ruin of the gate. Suddenly Malfons was there, greatsword blurring through the air. The Chapter Master moved with an agility in his Terminator armour that Koorland had never witnessed before. The ork dropped Koorland and kicked at Malfons, knocking the Chapter Master backwards, and snatched a fresh axe from its belt. It followed up with a powerful blow at Malfons.

The axe was of simple metal, but the strength of the ork was such that it bit deep into the ceramite cladding of Malfons' pauldron. The Chapter Master shouldered the ork aside, weathered a second strike, and swung his blade hard. The weapon cleft the ork's chest armour, slicing deep into muscle. With a howl of fury, the ork backhanded Malfons before he could attack again. Helm lenses shattered, Malfons faltered. An instant was all he gave the ork, but the creature grabbed it. The ork stamped down on Malfons' leg, pinning his foot in place, then it reached forward and clamped its fist around the Chapter Master's head.

As teleport blur smeared his sight, Koorland saw the ork rip Malfons' head free with one mighty wrench. Then he was in the blacklight glare of a teleport chamber, gas gushing all over him from the internal piping, and in his helm a voice announced, 'Teleport successful.'

The doors opened, and he clumped out. All around the deck, Black Templars emerged from other chambers. In several, dead warriors lay slumped in armour summoned back by the undeniable call of the *Abhorrence*'s machine-spirits.

'Bohemond, Thane, Issachar, Quesadra,' voxed Koorland. 'Malfons is dead.'

TWELVE

In pursuit of vengeance

The Black Templars cruiser *Obsidian Sky* shook as it came out of the warp, realspace engine stacks already burning bright. Five hundred metres of burnished black metal trailing the dying energies of the empyrean, it accelerated before the rift had closed, waiting on no nicety of post-transit protocols.

'Translation complete, Dreadnought-Marshal. We have arrived in the Klostra System,' called out Shipmaster Ericus.

The vision slit of Magneric's Dreadnought blazed, and it stood tall, pushed upright by actuators and hydraulics. Magneric was awake in an instant.

The Dreadnought-Marshal stumped around, the shoulders of the machine that housed his ruined body swaying. Relics of his earlier life rattled on the walker's armour.

'All hands to combat stations. Initiate full auspex scan. Open hails, send out our challenge. We shall not hide from them, call out their doom!' His voice boomed from his vox-speakers, brash as a Titan's war-horn.

'My lord, I am receiving a large amount of transmissions–' began the ship's Master Divulgatus from the craft's long vox-desks.

'Excellent!' roared Magneric. His power fist rotated in anticipation of the coming fight. 'All brothers, prepare for battle. Master Egredorum, prepare our transports. Track the source of the enemy's transmissions, we engage immediately.'

'But, my lord!' protested the Master Divulgatus. 'The transmissions are not those of the traitors, they are all ork.'

'I have multiple enemy contacts, half a million kilometre range and closing,' spoke the Master Augurum at the auspex array. 'Again, all ork energy signatures.'

Castellan Ralstan stepped forward to stand at the elbow of Magneric. 'Half a million kilometres?'

'It is at extreme range, my lord, but there are large numbers of them.'

'Marshal Magneric?' said the castellan.

Magneric let out a frustrated growl. 'How many times must our quarry slip through our fingers? Orks! I was informed that the Klostra System was the base of Kalkator's Great Company. Who shall atone for this failure in intelligence?'

'My lord, if I may,' said the Master Augurum, 'the auspex array is picking up residual vox-echo here, reflected from the system's radiation belts. There was a traitor presence on the planet until only a few days ago. No civilian messaging, all of it is Fourth Legion battle-cant.'

'Then it is over,' said Ralstan regretfully. 'The orks have done our duty for us. To our next crusade, brothers.'

'No!' bellowed Magneric, his torso spinning dangerously fast. The huge block of his sarcophagus leaned over, bringing the machine's glass eye level with the face of his second-in-command. 'It cannot be so, the Emperor has marked out Kalkator to die by my fist and my fist alone! I feel it. We departed Ostrom hot on the heels of Kalkator's dogs. If there is no longer sign of battle here, then they must have departed. Send for Honoured Navigator Pholax. I will speak with him as to their likely destination. In the meantime, have more power diverted to the auspex arrays. If by some small chance the greenskins have cheated us of our vengeance, I will be sure of it before moving on.'

'And the greenskins themselves, Magneric?'

'You would have us fear a few thousand orks?' Magneric boomed.

'A few *hundred* thousand, my lord,' corrected Ralstan. He held out his hand towards the massive doors leading to Magneric's inner sanctum. 'Perhaps we might continue this discussion on strategy in private?'

'Very well,' grumbled Magneric.

The command deck shook to the tread of his armoured feet. They went within Magneric's chamber. The doors hissed shut, and immediately they were isolated from the command deck Magneric rounded on Ralstan.

'You challenge my judgement? I, Magneric, hero of the Heresy? I, who remain in command despite my entombing? Who kept my own name when interred, when all others give up theirs?'

'Marshal,' said Ralstan calmly. 'It is my role to challenge you, as you well know.'

'"Nothing worthwhile is done without challenge, best to overcome it before plans are enacted,"' quoted Magneric.

'So said Sigismund,' said Ralstan.

'I do not quote our founder in support of your case, but against it!' said Magneric. 'Our plan was agreed, your opportunity to object has passed.'

'Perhaps. But lately you have taken against my naysaying, whenever performed.' Ralstan paced the empty expanse of the chamber. It had been stripped of everything, right back to the metal of the understructure, to accommodate the huge sepulchre the Dreadnought occupied when resting. Magneric refused to go to the forge-tombs, wishing to remain close to the centre of command at all times. 'I must again protest against your decision not to heed the High Marshal's order to return. The Last Wall has been invoked, and we should lend our strength to it, not spend our time harrying these traitors. There are greater issues at stake.'

'Our way is not that of the wall! Sigismund's oath is paramount. We are crusaders, not wall troops.'

'This is different, my lord.'

'It is not! We have the Iron Warriors at bay, we cannot allow them to dig themselves in, or we shall never pry them from their hiding place. We have to strike now. When they are finished, we shall embark upon this new crusade.'

'Magneric, your feelings are blinding you,' pleaded Ralstan. 'Vengeance is noble when enacted for the good of the Emperor. You seek vengeance for your own sake. You should rest. Frater Astrotechnicus Baldon told me that you are six months overdue a maintenance sleep.'

'So you speak for the scullions of Mars now!' boomed Magneric.

'You do our Brother-Techmarine dishonour to speak of him so.'

'And yet you question my honour!'

'I speak as your friend, your pupil, your admirer, my lord,' said Ralstan. Magneric's choler was becoming increasingly hard to douse, and Ralstan had to fight to hide his own ire. 'Your tomb was never intended to remain active for so long a time.'

Magneric's massive power fist came up and pointed threateningly. 'You undermine me, Castellan. Do not do so again.'

'At least speak with Chaplain Aladucos. If you will not hearken to me, listen to him.'

Magneric turned awkwardly, the short legs of the Dreadnought stamping clangorously on the deck. 'When I have Kalkator's severed head in my fist, when I have squeezed his treacherous brain into a paste, then I shall rest. Not before! By the Emperor, no matter what you or the others say, I have sworn my oath and I will honour it!'

The doors opened wide, and Magneric stamped back onto the bridge. Ralstan sighed with dissatisfaction, and followed.

Dzelenic IV had once had a name of its own. Now, it was marked upon the stellar charts of the Imperium by system and number alone. Kalkator was among the few who remembered what its inhabitants had called it, for he had witnessed its destruction.

A landscape of utter desolation slid beneath the keels of

the Iron Warriors Thunderhawks, the *Meratara* in the lead. They flew over a dry ocean basin subsumed into the wasteland of dunes that stretched from pole to pole. The seas were long since gone, stripped away by titanic weapons during the war against the False Emperor. Kalkator remembered it as a pleasant world, civilised and green. The forces of Terra had put paid to that.

The exposed ocean floor took a step up, marking the position of the ancient coast. The Thunderhawks swung around to the south, following the grim cliffs, footed only by a sea of dust. Savage storms blew up in what remained of the planet's atmosphere, turning the air orange with a perpetual haze.

City ruins sprouted from the dunes, emerging suddenly from the blurred sky, the only signs that anything living had ever been there at all. The long rectangles of docking piers extruded far out into the vanished sea, still visible beneath their shrouds of sand.

'North here, to the landing fields,' ordered Kalkator.

'As you command, warsmith,' confirmed the pilot, Lerontus.

A space port dominated the plain behind the city. Flat, dull grey landing aprons were swept clear by the ceaseless wind. A dry river bed wound past it towards a range of hills, exposed as the vein of a flayed corpse. Craters marred the ground, distinguishable only by their infill of windblown sand. Further cliffs edged the plain, the product of millions of years of geological processes that had been halted in an instant of fire.

'There, to the west. Set us down,' said Kalkator.

The *Meratara*'s ramp opened into a covering of powder soft as silk. The planet's death scream played still as constant gales, and over the last millennium they had worn the debris of the world's destruction to a fine loess. Kalkator donned his helmet before venturing outside, and bade his men do the same – the air would choke them by itself, but it was one peril among many. The ozone layer of Dzelenic IV had been stripped away, and the surface was bathed in stellar radiation from its parent star.

Behind the *Meratara* three other gunships squatted in the abiotic dirt of the dead world, engines cycling. The Iron Warriors had been caught too often recently to take any chances. Fifty Space Marines formed up beside the warsmith, a worryingly large proportion of his much diminished Great Company. They waited expectantly as Kalkator scanned the cliffs. The world was changed beyond recognition, its past topography a sketch in the dirt of its present. He could not see the entrance to the facility.

'Are you sure it is here, my lord?' said Caesax. 'This place is deader than a tomb. The cache could have been destroyed, or looted, or buried in a million tons of dirt.'

'Silence,' said Kalkator sharply, for he was well aware all that Caesax said was possible. 'You forget yourself.'

'Yes, warsmith,' muttered the other.

Caesax was close to what Kalkator might call a friend. Friendship was weakness. Brotherhood was all. Caesax's familiarity had encouraged him to test those boundaries recently.

Kalkator needed to keep him under control. They were all looking at him. Since Klostra had fallen, the hostility of his Great Company had grown. Although none yet outright defied him, how many of them could he truly count on, should it come to it? Best not to consider that eventuality. Deliver them victory, and they would follow. The iron of their loyalty would not be tested.

He finally found the worn aquila carved into the rock face, defaced fifteen centuries ago and further worn away by the ravages of the raging atmosphere. It was not where he had expected to find it. Kalkator had lived long enough to know that nothing was constant, not even stone. Not even iron.

'This way,' he said. He pointed with his left arm, the bionic. Let them see the iron in him clearly displayed. He marched through the debris of the world, a mix of desiccated biological matter and coarse sand torn from the bedrock, this material not yet aged enough to lose its sharp edges. Dzelenic IV's death was still fresh in planetary terms.

The sun came out from behind a flag of dirty yellow cloud, not vapour, but more detritus lofted high into the atmosphere. The star glared on them weakly, a sallow circle of light. Kalkator's warsuit informed him of climbing radiation with a series of idle clicks.

His men were still watching as he reached for a piece of stone. Remarkable, how the craftsmanship had held. The block stayed seated in position, its secret unrevealed.

He grasped it with both hands and yanked hard. The stone came free from its place with reluctance. He let it fall into the soft regolith. A lifeless panel lay behind, sticky with ancient oils and caked in microscopic particles. Kalkator reached out his arm, an interface dendrite snaking from his vambrace and into the access port. The small screen embedded above the key panel flickered green, then went out.

Kalkator stood back as a section of the cliff ten metres broad by four high receded with an almighty grinding clunk, and began a slow tracking to the right. Behind was a dark hangar, the smooth rockcrete floor and walls kept pristine by the planet's arid air. The door got halfway open before the power failed. Stacked pallets of transit crates covered in dirty plastek shrouds receded into the shadows in neat rows.

Dust was already snaking in from the outside when Kalkator issued his command.

'Empty it. Take everything.'

Collustrax pushed his way through another corroded door. Away from the hangar the complex was in bad shape, exhibiting seismic damage from the world-death. He passed down a stretch of corridor whose walls were shivered by cracks, his suit lights picking out ribbons of dust. He paused by a dessicated corpse dressed in the Imperial Army uniform of a regiment a thousand years forgotten. The bones of the man were still cloaked in skin, but so tight and dried they appeared to have been wrapped for transport in flaking plastek. When he toed the corpse the head rolled free.

He looked at the skull a moment, then stamped it flat.

'Section Lambda-8 clear,' he voxed. 'Nothing to report.'

The next door was jammed shut. He kicked it to pieces, his heavy boots powering through the corroded metal. It became loose, and he wrenched it free. An avalanche of dust poured out around his knees.

The corridor beyond was wider, an antechamber to

a larger hall perhaps. It was also bathed in light, and three-quarters full of sand. He raised his bolter and carefully covered the room. The ceiling was cracked from side to side by a wide crevasse that evidently reached the surface, for daylight penetrated all the way into the complex here, and dust whispered down in sheets. The door on the far side was buried in it.

'I cannot proceed further, the roof is breached and the corridor blocked with sand. It would take a day or more to dig through. No sign of supplies here.'

The vox crackled in response. 'Return to the hangar, brother.'

'Confirmed, sergeant,' said Collustrax. He keyed his vox off. 'A waste of time going further.'

He turned about and headed back the way he had come, deeper into the base. Doors he had opened before in his sweep hung wide. Most rooms were empty, those that were not held nothing useful to the Iron Warriors. Corpses, paper that fell to pieces when disturbed, dead cogitators.

He strode on with purpose, making no attempt to go quietly. There was no one to hear him.

Suddenly he stopped and backed up. He looked down, the lights attached to his suit bathing the floor in wan yellow light. The dust was scuffed by his passage, but there was something else.

Another set of footprints overlaid his own.

He shut his light off, brought up a thermal overlay on his helm display. The corridor reappeared as a grainy pict of false colour. His own footprints were a dull blue against the near black of the floor. The interloper's were a fading green, more recent.

'Sergeant Ostrakam. Collustrax. I've found something.'

'Report.'

'There's something in here with us. Footprints. Booted, large.'

The second line of footprints went into a room Collustrax had investigated on the way up. He moved against the wall, and leaned in, bolter first.

'Nothing there.' He stood back again. 'I will–'

A ringing blow against his helmet sent him sprawling into the wall. A blackened knife blade skidded off the metal. Collustrax jerked his shoulder back, meeting a solid body that barely gave. He swung around, but a meaty hand grabbed his pauldron and hurled him against the opposite wall. A huge ork stood over him, a pair of primitive light-intensification goggles strapped over its eyes. With calm efficiency Collustrax brought his bolter up to blow out its heart and lungs, but his assailant grabbed it and ripped it out of his hand with amazing strength, stamping Collustrax into the ground as he sought to rise.

'Orks! There are orks in the complex. There are–'

The ork drove down with its knife, a piece of metal as long as a man's torso and thick as three fingers. For all its unwieldiness the ork used it deftly, and the ridiculous breadth of it was ground down on one side to a wicked edge.

The point caught in the seal where his helmet joined his breastplate and was driven through it by brute strength, into the space behind Collustrax's collarbone. The ork threw itself forward with its full weight, pushing the sword-length

knife in with both hands so that it pierced both the Iron Warrior's hearts.

For Collustrax, the Long War was over.

Sergeant Ostrakam saluted Kalkator. 'My lord Kalkator, Brother Collustrax is slain by orks. The complex is compromised.'

Kalkator regarded the emptying hangar. They had recovered perhaps half of the supplies, armour spares, bolt-rounds, weapons. Most of it was sealed in oil-filled containers, and perfectly serviceable. Kalkator tallied what they had recovered mentally, deciding if they could afford to leave the remaining supplies.

'Any word from the *Palimodes*?' he called to his master vox-operator. 'What news from orbit?'

'I cannot raise the ship, my lord.'

Why would this be easy? One cruiser lost, two outposts, half his Great Company. Kalkator's week had been disastrous.

'Caesax! Take half the company, secure the hangar rear. Derruo, take four squads outside. Shift the landing site ten kilometres out, somewhere clear where we can't be ambushed. *Meratara* will ferry the supplies, let the others take them to orbit. Unloading and reloading will take extra time, but we cannot risk the gunships, and a few more crates of supplies is better than no more. As soon as you raise him, have Attonax send down more servitors and brothers to speed the extraction, both here and at site beta. Ostrakam, what indication of numbers?'

'None, my lord. None of the other scouts report anything. It will not be alone.'

'They never are,' said Kalkator. 'We have no indication of an infestation of the planet. It may be a scouting group. Send my order to Attonax. Intensify scans of the surrounding void. If there's a ship out there, we must find it. In the meantime, redouble our efforts. I want every scrap of usable materiel stripped from this depot and aboard the *Palimodes* before they find us.'

'Too late, my lord! I have Attonax.'

'Patch his vox-feed through to me.'

'Yes, my lord.'

Attonax's voice came through crisply, boosted by the nuncio-vox of Kalkator's master operator over the angry grumble of the planet's tortured magnetosphere. 'Fifteen contacts emerging from the shadow of the third moon, my lord. They have seen us.'

'No more?'

'No, warsmith. It appears to be a scouting group, ork pirate scum looking for easy kills or planets to plunder. They are weak, and will not be on our position for two hours, give or take.'

Gunfire sounded from deep in the complex. Reports of ork engagements on three fronts came in on a sudden wave of vox-noise.

'We will not abandon the supplies! Attonax, keep the planet between you and the orks. Begin evacuation immediately. Everyone else to the rear of the hall.'

Kalkator unclipped his pistol and unsheathed his sword. His servo-arm unfurled as he strode past the serfs sweating in their rebreathers as they dragged out supply pallets on pneumatic jacks. 'I tire of running from these creatures.'

THIRTEEN

Iron and faith

Like a shark following the scent of blood in the water, the *Obsidian Sky* came hard out of interplanetary night, streaking towards the fourth planet of the Dzelenic System, the battle there lighting up its auspexes and augurs.

'Well?' said Magneric.

'We have them in our sights, Marshal,' reported Ericus eagerly. 'There are orks here, but a paltry number.'

The oculus was closed for battle, and so Ericus ordered the hololith lit. The display burst into life, bathing the faces of all aboard the command deck in dancing light. Auspex data crowded a true pict of the planet. A strike cruiser stood embattled in the sky over the dead world. Explosions in miniature flared in the space of the bridge as ork attack craft detonated messily.

'Behold, the *Palimodes*,' said Ericus.

'I recognise it of old,' growled Magneric. 'At last, Kalkator shall face justice!'

'Your orders, my lord?' asked Ericus.

'We should stand back and watch the orks destroy them,' advised Ralstan, 'then slay the surviving orks. That would be the most tactically astute action. We might then locate the Iron Warriors on the surface, and deal with them at our leisure. If we attack now, we shall find ourselves with not one foe, but two.'

'And afford Kalkator the luxury of escape?' bellowed Magneric. 'No! The craven traitors will surely flee as soon as they catch sight of us. We will attack both ground forces and the *Palimodes* simultaneously. Prepare all drop-craft. We assault the surface immediately. Sword Brother Rolans?' ·

Sword Brother Rolans stepped forward, the black of his armour thick with the red crosses of the Black Templars veterans. 'My lord Dreadnought-Marshal,' responded Rolans.

'Take one-third of the crusade. Choose your own men. Equip them for ship-to-ship combat. I bestow upon you the honour of assaulting and taking the *Palimodes*.'

'It will be done gratefully, my lord,' said Rolans.

'Master Ericus, you will drive through the orks attacking the *Palimodes*, and bring the ship within boarding range. We shall take back their ship, purify it, and re-induct it into the rightful service of our Lord the Emperor.'

'Praise be!' shouted the Black Templars and their bondsmen.

The shout of praise was silent on Ralstan's lips. Misgivings plagued him.

'My lord,' he said tentatively. 'I beg of you not to attack two enemies at once. Let them expend their strength upon one another. See here, Magneric. The orks are deploying aircraft and personnel to the surface.'

Ralstan had the hololithic display zoom in to a fat ork carrier craft. Its sides were riddled with hangars and launch tubes. From these a steady stream of smaller ships issued, turning downwards into the planetary gravity well. 'If there are no orks on the ground yet, soon there will be thousands.'

'The orks are of no concern!' roared Magneric. He turned his massive suit of armour on his lieutenant. Magneric raised his vox-amplifiers to maximum. 'All battle-brothers proceed to drop-craft. Heed my commands, gunnery control. Upon flyover of the Iron Warriors' planetside positions, find and target the transports of the traitors. Destroy the ships. Strand the Iron Warriors, so that we might face them blade to blade. They will taste our anger – no swift demise in fire for them! I will see them beg for forgiveness. Kalkator will not escape me this time. Shipmaster Ericus, move to engage the *Palimodes* directly.'

'As you command, my lord,' said Ericus.

'My lord Magneric...' said Ralstan.

'Castellan Ralstan!' said Magneric, his metallic voice enthused by the prospect of battle. 'The way prescribed by our founder is always forward! We shall not hang back like jackals while the lions fight! You have your orders. With me unto battle, bold soldiers of the Emperor! We shall destroy these paltry orks, and take the *Palimodes*, and return to our Chapter with it as a trophy of war! I go now to ready myself for drop in the basilicus.' He leaned over Ralstan, and lowered his voice. 'I will brook no more dissent, castellan, be warned.'

Magneric thundered out of the command deck.

'By the will of Magneric, make so his orders!' commanded

Ralstan. Forcing down his own disquiet, he began to make preparations for planetstrike.

A squawking of surprised messages burst from the vox-station as the *Obsidian Sky* slid down towards the *Palimodes*.

'Master Divulgatus, silence that noise.'

'Aye, shipmaster, initiating wide-band vox-jamming now.'

Ericus leaned forward, the weight of the cables plugged into his neck shifting on his shoulder. 'We will pay no heed to the words of the traitors. Open fire on the orks and prepare to clear the way. Prow lance batteries to mark these targets and fire upon my command.' He indicated his priorities on the hololith. 'Primary gun batteries sweep the flanks. Spinal turrets fire at will. Scour the void. We shall shield Lord Magneric's landing and then proceed to take the *Palimodes*.'

'Drop-tubes loaded,' reported the Master Egredorum.

The ship's void shields flickered as the first of the orks noticed their new foe, and turned their guns upon them. Energy beams hit out first, cutting like searchlights across the dark. Across the command deck, bells tolled gently, bringing soft notice of the clouds of deadly projectiles following on behind.

Ericus settled himself into his command throne. He reached out and grasped his sword; a servant of the Black Templars always fought with a weapon in his grasp.

The command deck, rarely full of needless chatter, took on a focused air. Orders and commentary were the only words spoken. Servitors sighed and muttered quietly. Cogitators clacked in their housings. The crew of the ship was minimal, most of the work done by mind-wiped servitors or vat-born things that had never known a name, plugged directly into the ship's systems. The fifty unaltered men who manned the command deck were sombre with the privilege bestowed on them.

'Range to the *Palimodes* six thousand kilometres and closing,' relayed the Master Augurum.

'Open hangar bays and drop-tube shielding. Drop countdown commencing in three, two, one. Mark.' The number 120 appeared on the hololith and began to rapidly count down, its colouring turning from green to red as it approached zero.

'Turret pins released,' said the Ordinatum Secundus. 'Main ordnance ready for firing. Lance batteries one through four are charged and await your command, Master Ericus.'

Fifty years had passed since Ericus had fallen at the second obstacle in his bid to become a member of the Black Templars. Despite his high suitability, his genetic code proved incompatible with the Chapter gene-seed. The memory of that day haunted him forever, and yet here he was, armed and glorious, a mighty warship at his command. The lives of his masters were under his care. There was no greater duty.

'For the glory of the Emperor, launch,' he said.

'Praise be,' intoned the crew as one.

The distant rumble of rockets firing vibrated the deck plating. The ship shifted infinitesimally at the release of such large amounts of mass.

'Correctional thrusters firing,' reported the Master

Egredorum. The ship pushed back against the jettisoning of its drop-vehicles. 'Our lieges are away. Five minutes to touchdown. Praise be.'

Light flared in the hololith as an ork assault craft exploded. The *Palimodes*, shields twinkling with orkish fire, had rotated about its centre, presenting its stern to the *Obsidian Sky*. This was a ship's most vulnerable aspect, but they were close to the horizon – one good burn would put them out of sight, leaving the Black Templars entangled with the orks.

'The Iron Warriors are running. Proceed towards the *Palimodes*,' ordered Ericus. 'We will accomplish Magneric's orders. My lord Sword Brother Rolans, you may prepare your boarding party. Helm, run the traitors down.'

Kalkator gripped the ork's head in his servo-claw and squeezed. The thick skull cracked, deforming the ork's already hideous alien features. Still it fought on, until Kalkator jammed his bolt pistol into its mouth and blew the back of its head off.

The last few pallets were being removed hurriedly from the hangar, the rest having been dragged out under fire. Ork bodies lay about the hall, intermixed with luckless serfs and servitors caught in the crossfire. Otherwise, casualties were light. Kalkator had lured the orks into the hangar, where they were pinned between carefully planned fields of fire and gunned down without mercy.

The orks were odd specimens. They had the look of infiltration specialists to them, executed in that clumsy, slightly comical way the orks had with everything they did. Their weapons were oversized, the camo patterns they wore jarring, but their faces were blackened, their weapons burned dark, and their equipment – nightsight goggles, grenades, charges and the like – seemed serviceable enough. As his scorn rose, he reminded himself they had successfully infiltrated the complex.

Kalkator had his squads report in. No more contacts with the enemy were reported.

The orks were dead. After several dispiriting days, Kalkator's spirits were uplifted.

'Bordan, raise the *Palimodes*!' he ordered. 'All squads prepare for immediate extraction.' He strode out of the hangar back into the pale day of Dzelenic IV. The last of the supplies were being loaded into the Thunderhawks, the undersides of the ships glowing orange with repeated, rapid ascensions and re-entries.

'I cannot raise the *Palimodes*, my lord,' said Bordan.

Kalkator tapped his gun impatiently against his leg. 'Then try again.' The space beyond the clouds was lit occasionally by the false-lightning of low-orbital battle. 'Surely they have not been overwhelmed?'

'No, my lord, there is a blanket denial broadcast preventing communication.'

'From the orks?' said Kalkator.

'I cannot discern the location of the broadcast, my lord. It could be the orks.'

'Or...' said Kalkator. He fell silent a moment. 'Magneric,' he whispered. 'We will ascend and deal with the problem at source. Board the transports!'

Kalkator marched up the gangway of the *Meratara*, his serfs, weaklings before his armoured form, scurrying out of his way.

His warriors fell back out of the emptied complex, covering their fellows squad by squad. For a moment Kalkator was transported by the efficiency of his Great Company, back to a time when they fought for a master other than themselves.

He slapped his palm against the ship, quashing his nostalgia. Iron Warriors ran up the ramp as it closed. The engines whined loudly. Turning from the dead world, Kalkator went to the flight deck.

'Lerontus.'

'My lord,' acknowledged the pilot.

'Remove us from this place.'

The ground dropped away, rapidly becoming a hazy caramel nothingness, a void that could contain anything. Kalkator stared at it, remembering the world it had been.

A sudden jolt brought him back to the present.

'Incoming fire!' shouted Lerontus.

'Origin point?'

'Orbit, Lord Kalkator! Lance strike!' Lerontus grunted and heaved hard on his flight stick. A beam of coruscating energy stabbed down, glassing the ground one hundred metres ahead of them. The *Meratara* bucked as it rode out the shock wave. The *Adamantine* was not so blessed. Its starboard wing trailed streamers of fire, loosened panels shaking in the airstream, and it began a rapid emergency descent. Lerontus dodged the damaged craft, sending the *Meratara* leapfrogging over it and accelerating ahead, leaving the *Adamantine* to disappear into the haze-cloaked dunes. Another blast seared through the sky, carving a pillar of clear air through the smog. Thunderous shock waves boomed out after each strike.

'Standard suppression pattern,' grunted Lerontus, piloting the Thunderhawk through the agitated air. 'The orks are copying Imperial fire protocols.'

Kalkator's boots locked to the floor, and he bent forward to peer out of the top of the Thunderhawk's canopy.

'They are not orks. That was a precursor barrage to a drop assault,' said Kalkator. He pointed upward to where the clouds swirled around the track of the orbital strikes, discharge-lightning crawling along their undersides. The beam strikes cut out, and the sky lit up with multiple flashes. 'Magneric must be hot with fury at my continued liberty, if he tries to hit gunships in atmosphere with lance fire,' he said. 'If he tracked the others to the Ostrom System, he will have gone to Klostra, and from there, he will have come here.'

'Sounds like Magneric,' said Caesax. 'He is tenacious.'

'It is Magneric, almost certainly,' said Kalkator. 'He has dogged my footsteps since the end of Horus' war. I hear he continues his crusade from beyond the grave. So you can imagine, Caesax, it will take more than an ork Waaagh! to dissuade him.'

'I do not need to imagine it, my lord. They are coming.'

Bright meteors burst through the clouds, streaking groundward to the east. They came down rapidly, their snowy vapour trails scoring the yellow-brown sky. 'We must leave. I will see if Vorstrex and his command can be recovered.' Kalkator switched his vox-channel, seeking out the downed *Adamantine*. He cursed at discovering the range of his battleplate's vox insufficient, and switched his communications feed through the Thunderhawk's own systems.

A wider world of sound greeted him: the garbled chatter of the Black Templars' communications, overlaid atop the hissing of the dead world's voice. He scanned through multiple channels, seeking out his comrades.

A blip, and a tumble of shouted squad communication burst into his earpieces.

'Vorstrex, this is Kalkator. Respond.' There was no reply. Kalkator tried again, without success. It was clear the leading sergeant of the men aboard the *Adamantine* could not hear him. Kalkator heard him shouting urgent orders. The banging of bolter fire crackled over the vox, and with it he heard the roaring of orks.

'It appears there are now orks also upon the planet in large numbers,' said Kalkator leadenly. 'They attack Vorstrex.'

'There is more, warsmith,' said Lerontus. 'Enemy gunships have deployed and will move against us. They will be deep enough into the atmosphere to begin pursuit and intercept within five minutes.'

The tactical display of the Thunderhawk was crowded with icons denoting the Black Templars forces. Out of the window, curling contrails pulled away from the gracefully curved descent lines of the drop pods.

'Five of them, and we are just the two,' said Kalkator.

'Long odds,' said Caesax.

'I have endured worse. Alter course. Put some distance between us and the Black Templars. Head for that ruin.' Kalkator pointed at a squat building jutting from the sands some ten kilometres away. 'We shall make our stand there. Let them blunt their ire upon a sea of orks. When they are done, our guns shall be waiting.'

* * *

'Prepare forward lance batteries!' commanded Ericus. 'Spinal turret array stand by for my command. Reopen the oculus.'

'Compliance,' mumbled a servitor. Motors grumbled as they pulled the massive blast shields back from the window.

Ericus looked from the oculus to the hololithic tactical display. On the display the *Obsidian Sky*'s immediate environs appeared crowded with combatants, swarms of green signifiers clustering around both Imperial and traitor vessels. Through the armourglass of the grand window, space appeared anything but: a huge expanse of black, the light of the stars outshone by the albedo glare of Dzelenic IV. Near space sparkled with dancing motes, all that was visible to the human eye of their xenos enemies. Beyond this shifting cloud, the *Palimodes* was a punctuation mark of light.

The command deck was a murmur of idiot servitor queries and reports, overlaid with the terse, efficient battle talk of the Chapter servants.

'We are within optimum range, shipmaster. Shall I give the order to open fire?'

'Negative. Hold fire. We will not be drawn into a duel, but shall force our munitions down their throats at point-blank range. Then we shall unleash our masters upon the traitors aboard.'

'As you command, shipmaster.'

A bell rang. Servitors gabbled moaning alarms. 'Multiple orkish contacts closing from planetary east,' reported the Master Augurum.

'Steady as she goes,' ordered Ericus.

'Range two thousand kilometres and closing. We are gaining on the *Palimodes*,' said the Master Augurum.

'Wait for it!' demanded Ericus. He leaned forward in his command throne, leather gloves squeaking on each other as he massaged his hands over his sword hilt.

'Shipmaster! More orkish vessels approach from planetary north. Interceptor and bomber wings launched. They're coming in fast. Contact in twenty seconds. Nineteen, eighteen...'

Alarms clamoured. 'Alert, alert,' groaned a choir of hissing mechanical voices. 'Boarders detected. Decks ninety-seven, forty-two and six. Alert, alert, boarders detected.'

'Long-range teleport, origin unknown,' said the Master Augurum.

'Was there any warning?' snapped Ericus.

'Negative, sir, they just came out of nowhere.'

'Seal all bulkheads. Serjeants-at-arms are hereby given permission to open the armouries and distribute weaponry to the ship crew. All Chapter warrior bondsmen stand ready. Armsmen to the affected sites,' said Ericus.

'Shipmaster, this is Sword Brother Rolans.' Rolans' sonorous, transhuman voice rolled out across the command deck. 'We shall postpone our boarding attempt. It will avail us naught if we take the *Palimodes* and our own vessel is overrun by the orks. I am moving to engage boarders.'

'Allow my men to take care of the problem, my lord,' said Ericus. 'We are within boarding torpedo range of the *Palimodes*.'

'There are too many,' countered Rolans. 'Your men will be destroyed. We will show them the Emperor's displeasure at first hand.'

'Very well, my lord,' said Ericus, but Rolans had already gone.

'Bomber wing approaching. They have launched torpedoes.'

A flight of crude orkish fighters soared over the spine of the *Obsidian Sky*, chased by streams of glowing tracer fire. A moment later the ship shook. A score of bombers hurtled past, weaving between each other recklessly as they dodged the *Obsidian Sky*'s anti-interceptor fire. One disintegrated into a cloud of glowing scraps. The rest were away.

'Damage control?' asked Ericus.

'Nothing to report. Negative impact,' said the Master Divulgatus.

'Shields?'

'The void shields took the brunt of it, shipmaster,' said the Master Scutum. 'All reading within optimal limits.'

'Shipmaster, the northern and eastern groups of orkish ships are gaining.'

'What is your command, sir?' asked the Master Ordinatum.

Ericus glanced at the tactical displays. Ork ships closed on two horizons, coming fast and low around Dzelenic IV. Four cruiser-class in each group. The Imperial ship had the advantage of range; orkish projectiles were inaccurate and unreliable at distance. Up close they would be devastating.

'Emperor forgive me, I pray that Lord Magneric shall understand my actions, and be merciful,' said Ericus quietly. 'Abort attack run on the *Palimodes*! Provide gun crew with new orders, Franzek. Kill the orks. Destroy their ships before they can close.'

'Conveying new firing solutions to all batteries. Solutions conveyed. Open fire.'

The *Obsidian Sky* quaked under the release of its guns.

Lance beams burst through space. Cannons spoke, scattering high-velocity chaff around the vessel in a razored net that caught ork fighters and rent them to pieces.

'Port broadside, engage eastern ork group. Thin their numbers,' ordered Ericus.

'Aye, sir!'

The ship rocked as the port guns fired. Twenty seconds later, the lead ork cruiser of the eastern group flew into the mass of projectiles. It burst apart at the seams, flickering energy and fire crawling over the broken pieces for a moment before it went dark. The aft of the hull spun away, connecting with the cruiser following and severely damaging it. The remaining two ork cruisers clumsily split, getting in each other's way.

'Shipmaster. We have two cruisers coming at us astern!'

'Come about, port side,' ordered Ericus. 'Batteries and lances stand ready.' The ship's engines rumbled and metal sang at the sudden course correction, played upon by the gravity of the planet and its own momentum.

A klaxon blurted out a mournful wail. 'New contacts appearing everywhere! Behind the moon, from near space... Dozens of them. They must have been waiting, engines dark. We're surrounded!'

'A trap?' said Ericus incredulously. He stared at the hololith as augur data was fed into its cogitators. New contacts sprang into life, bright red, a net around his ships. Ork ships now approached from three quadrants at once, only the *Palimodes* standing between them. 'Port battery open fire on northern group. Keep them off the stern,' Ericus commanded.

'Fresh ork cruiser group coming aft!' shouted the Master Augurum.

'*Palimodes* is mirroring our movement and is coming about also!' added his second.

The *Palimodes'* main engine stack dimmed. All along its sides flared the ice-white sparks of braking jets. The nose dipped, carrying it to the very edge of the atmosphere. As it dived, it lumbered around and turned on its side a little, ignoring the swarm of ork attack craft pressing it from all sides, and presented its full broadside to the oncoming prow and keel of the *Obsidian Sky*.

'They're preparing to fire!' called Franzek.

'Up thirty degrees. Concentrate anti-interceptor fire to ventral aspect, support anti-munition cannons, or they'll tear the guts out of us!' shouted Ericus, half rising from his seat, his link cables tugging at his augmetics.

Cannon muzzles ripple-flashed up the length of the *Palimodes'* port side.

Glinting shells sped across the void.

'Time to impact five, four, three, two, one...'

'*Brace, brace, brace!*'

No impact came. Ericus glanced at the display. Red reticules spun past the icon denoting the *Obsidian Sky*, heading into the ork ships chasing them. They blinked rapidly before impact. The ork ship icons flashed, and vanished.

'They are firing on the orks!' reported the Master Augurum.

Space was alive with explosions and the burning light of high-energy weapons fire. The main hololithic display blinked thickly with yet more orkish attack craft.

'Close oculus shutters. Replace holo-display with true

representation of the battlespace. We will concentrate our efforts on the orks. See if you can raise the shipmaster of the *Palimodes*. If they are not going to fire upon us, we will offer them a truce, for now.'

'Marshal Magneric, shipmaster...'

'I am shipmaster,' said Ericus. 'It is my responsibility. Rather he has a ship to return to and a shipmaster to execute, than no ship at all.'

FOURTEEN

The dead of Mars

Clementina Yendl disembarked from the transit tube, the dusty windows of the station affording her a view of the facilities clustered about Pavonis Mons. Low volcanic slopes rose imperceptibly, a bulge in the land that somehow managed to attain fourteen kilometres of altitude at its apex. Much of the mountain's shield was covered with manufactoria of immeasurable size, stepped ranks that marched ever upward until they passed out of the Martian atmosphere and into the airless void. One of the great Tharsian forge temples soared over its attendant factories, in its shadow the barracks of a Titan Legion. Pavonis Mons looked like the rest of Tharsis, but there was a sombre air about this part of the Tharsis quadrangle, and rumours of a secret buried deep. Yendl knew it was more than hearsay. Yendl knew a lot of things. No data-stream was safe from the infocyte.

She passed down the platform and out through crowd-flow barriers. Machines inside the baroque pillars kept watch on the teeming citizenry of Mars. They read her implants, chiming acceptance of her signum codes. Yendl hurried down steps, arms hugging her data-slate to her chest in perfect imitation of a lowly acolyte late in performing her errands.

Wide doors opened into a wider hall. A curved plex-glass roof, its panels thick with the leavings of the last great dust storm, showed the pale blue of the Martian sky fading to yellow towards the horizon. A thick brown line of smog trapped by atmospheric temperature striation formed an artificial boundary between them, dividing one from the other definitively.

The stairs plunged deeper into the Martian world-city down a square shaft, and Yendl followed them for dozens of flights. A barrier divided the stairs into two, the left side for those going down, the right for those coming up. Cyber-constructs buzzed through the air, using the shaft's middle as their own highway.

Only lower-ranking followers of the Omnissiah used the steps, but they numbered in the billions, and examples of all of Mars' strange humanity could be seen there. Clanking servitors carrying giant burdens caused chokepoints, slowing the descent to a crawl, their monotasked minds ignorant of the curses and shouts of those they delayed. A file of electro-priests passed upwards singing a buzzing electric song to their god, their blinded eyes and tattooed blue skin all but concealed by the grey robes and hoods they wore. Adepts of less humble station clattered about on skittish spider sedans, using the weight of their machines to push through the throngs. Yendl pushed also, muttering to herself angrily about delays and systems failures, often checking the chronograph set into the upper lip of her data-slate with a frown.

'Please, please, let me through,' she said, 'or Magos Saultis will be angry with me again!'

Hers was but one of a million small problems harboured by those tramping the stairs, but a few allowed her to pass. She slipped around them, vox-augmetics chittering effusive binharic thanks into the noosphere, and vanished into the crowd. Just another lowly adept, one among teeming multitudes.

Ordinarily Yendl would not have drawn even this small measure of attention to herself. Her temple's way was to watch, rarely to act, to blend seamlessly into whatever place they found themselves in. To be a face in a crowd that no one would remember.

Time was short. Tracking phages were close to sniffing out her data-thieves parasiting the Martian world-mind. Verraux had arranged to meet with her the day before, but had not arrived at their rendezvous or contacted her since. Given a few more hours Yendl could have divined her fate with certainty, but she did not need to. Red Haven had been compromised.

Already she had begun to compile probable vectors for their discovery. Urquidex was the most prominent, but not likely, for the information he had provided her had been extremely sensitive. If she survived this mission, she would pay him a visit, after Pavonis Mons.

The Martians had hidden their intentions well, but not well enough. Another experimental undertaking had been established in the volcano's laboratoria. The same encrypted signifiers that were attached to the matter transportation experiments had been buried deep within the encoded data packets regarding this new development. Vast amounts of something were being delivered, but she had yet to ascertain what. The noosphere would only give up so many of its secrets. Yendl was forced to act, her task given greater impetus by Verraux's disappearance.

At roughly the level of Mars' original surface, now buried under a kilometre of plascrete, Yendl's exit from the stairs presented itself, one of many hundreds of large archways. She had to fight her way from the stairs, deftly enough to get free of them and through the door, but not so well that she drew attention to herself. She stiffened as she approached the hollow eye sockets of a bioscanner servitor guarding the way.

'Proceed,' it said leadenly to an adept ahead of her. 'Proceed,' to the next. 'Proceed.' A pale green scanning beam passed over her face. 'Proceed,' it said. The man behind her pushed impatiently.

She hurried away, an endless litany of 'Proceed' following her down the corridor.

Yendl went deeper into the hive factories of Pavonis Mons, following obscure ways until she was mostly alone on dusty paths trodden only by slack-mouthed servitors and a few robed adepts. None of these furtive figures challenged her. There were thousands of sub-cults and power structures within the Adeptus Mechanicus, a failing she was singularly thankful for.

She came to her last legitimate path, a narrow alleyway whose sheer sides stretched away into dark obscurity high overhead. She paused by a sealed access door, her hood over her face. A sole servitor stumped on by, power plant whistling. She waited until it had disappeared into the gloom. Sure she was alone, she acted quickly, prising open a maintenance hatch and stuffing her adept's robes inside where they fell into the unknowable spaces between the walls. Her body beneath gleamed with shiny synskin. Pouches crowded her thighs and waist. At her hips were a pistol and a trio of long stilettos. Her posture straightened, her augmetics reconfigured. The tech-adept was gone and the Assassin was revealed.

She primed her data-slate for a full wipe, waited for its compliance light to blink green, then snapped it in two. She withdrew the memory crystal and ground it to powder under her heel. The remains of the data-slate followed her robes, rattling away from discovery. She scooped up the powdery remains of the crystal and dusted half of that down the hatch also, retaining the rest for disposal elsewhere. It was perfectly possible the means to reconstitute the device existed somewhere within the vaults of techno-arcana that covered Mars. Her disguise dealt with, she flexed her fingers, extruding feathered access probes from her digital implants. The door slid open noiselessly, revealing an access corridor lit by dull yellow lumen panels. Glancing around herself one last time, she slipped out of sight.

Crammed into a tiny ventilation duct, Yendl watched a storage hall through a grille. Yet another twenty-wheeled hauler pulled up to a hissing halt. Tracked lifters manned by the implanted torsos of servitors swarmed it, acting in concert to lift the massive transit container from the flatbed and take it away to be stacked. Unburdened, the transport drew away, its place in the loading bay taken by another. Yendl frowned. She scanned the warehouse, and saw nothing more threatening than servitors of various kinds trudging about their endless labours.

She shuffled back along the ventilation conduit on her hands and knees, seeking out a point of egress. There were no hatches or large panels that could be prised free. She probed in the semi-darkness at the joins between the plates, eventually finding a tiny access portal less than a third of a metre on each side. The bolts securing it she undid in short order, and it fell to the floor two metres below with a quiet *bang*.

Taking a deep breath, Yendl forced her arm out and pushed her head after, the lip of the metal scraping her forehead as she twisted to fit through. Shoving with her toes, she attempted to push herself out, but she would not fit. The corridor her head protruded into was deserted, but clean, and clean meant heavily trafficked. From the corner of her eye she could see the end, a doorless aperture opening directly into the warehouse. She had to get in there, to see what was in the containers.

Taking another, deeper breath, she made her muscles in her back spasm violently, dislocating her shoulder.

Now she could fit.

Yendl wriggled through, blanking out the pain as her shoulder emerged through the hole. She let her left arm flop down. With her upper torso out, the rest slithered out easily. She executed an inelegant somersault and landed on her feet. She waited, poised, one hand on the pistol at her waist. The bustle of the warehouse continued uninterrupted. Holding her shoulder, she went to the wall, then slammed it into the metal. The bones relocated themselves with a painful pop. She rotated her shoulder. A good reset – the discomfort was manageable.

Drawing pistol and blade, she crept noiselessly into the warehouse.

Another of the great weaknesses of the Martian empire was that so many of its citizens were mindless drones. Such an eagerness to lobotomise played into the hands of the likes of the Officio Assassinorum, whose operatives could move far more freely than on other worlds within the Imperium; the servitors simply ignored anything that fell outside their programming. The warehouse was crowded with cyber-constructs of all kinds. She dodged between them as they rattled about, and went to the door of one of the shipping containers. The lock was sigma grade, heavily shielded. She could get it open, of course, but that would bring with it a risk of detection, and would take time.

She looked about. They could not just be stacking containers somewhere they must be unloading them. From where she was situated she could see no open containers or other types of servitor that might lead her to her goal, so she looked upwards. The stacks were tall and she would fare better from the top. Holstering her pistol and placing her knife between her teeth, she clambered up the smooth side of the transit containers. Once up, she ran and jumped from stack to stack, always landing silently, gun ready for interception. A hunch drew her to the rear of the warehouse, and there fortune favoured her.

At the foot of the stack, the doors to a container were open. A file of servitors carrying something like casualty biers were marching inside, their stretchers empty, and returning with them full – massive, bulky objects hidden in white plastek sacks. These servitors too seemed to be unsupervised, so she leapt from the top of the containers, weak Martian gravity allowing her to fall several metres with the lightest of impacts. She hurried to the line of servitors and fell in beside them. As usual they ignored her. They trudged towards a door out of the warehouse, where a dingy corridor led away. A quick slip of her knife opened one of the sealed bags, and she bent down to peer inside, still moving alongside the servitors.

Inside was the naked corpse of an ork. The smell of it was staggering, and she switched to breathing through her mouth. A fat pink tongue lolled between dagger teeth of yellow ivory. Its red eyes were half closed, lifeless and dull. Massive craters pocked its flesh, and the left arm was missing. Bolt-wounds. She stepped back, letting the flow of servitors pass her as she moved back up the line to the container. Inside were dozens of shelves arrayed like bunks, transit webbing hanging loose over the sides where they had been emptied. At the rear of the container a refrigeration unit blinked running lights from red to green and back again. White vapour, smelling strongly of methalon, pooled on the floor.

Yendl ran through the calculations in her head, balancing up the size of the warehouse with the number of containers and transit cradles... She drew in a sharp breath.

Over *ten thousand* orks.

'What by the Throne do they want ten thousand dead orks for?' she whispered. She had to inform Vangorich. She had to make contact.

Yendl sneaked through the comings and goings of servitors. There were so many she almost did not recognise the skitarii for what they were until it was too late. So much metal melded to flesh. Telling the autonomous servants of the priesthood apart from their slaves was nigh-on impossible.

At the last second she noticed them, diving behind a container as a bullet buzzed past her face, setting her internal rad sensors screaming.

'Halt! Halt! Unauthorised personnel, halt!' screeched a harsh metallic voice. Iron feet pounded the plascrete of the warehouse floor, coming at her from both sides of the container stack.

The first skitarius found an energy blast waiting for it. Yendl had studied the endless variations of the cybernetic warriors exhaustively, and knew the weak points of each. It was thrown backwards by the blast of her pistol, an exotic relic of the great Heresy war, tangling the legs of the one coming behind it. Yendl was already moving backwards, directly into the path of those coming up the other side. She sidestepped the next bullet coming for her, a movement that brought her around the barrel of the skitarius' gun. She grabbed the stock, preventing the cyborg from repositioning its weapon, shooting the one behind with her pistol, then the one behind that. The gears of the skitarius' mechanical arms clicked with effort to push Yendl aside, but her slender augmetic arms were supplemented with hidden fibre bundles, and her stance was immovable.

Two further skitarii rounded the rear of the container. The first's visor met her elbow, driving shattered glass and metal into its brain. The second got a bullet from the gun of its comrade when Yendl pivoted on the spot and yanked hard, mashing the trapped skitarius' finger against the trigger. Only that one remained. She wrenched the gun away, threw the skitarius aside and shot it three times, in the chest, head and reactor unit.

She made sure they were all dead and their datacores shattered, then she was away.

Alarms rang. Before anyone could respond, Yendl had gone.

A steady procession of foot traffic flowed along the Trans-Tharsis Highway's pedestrian strip. The lights of giant vehicles blurred past in a roar of colour and sound.

Clementina Yendl arranged her new disguise, a robe taken from a menial now dead and never to be found. She adjusted her posture, becoming once again the low-ranking adept, her augmetics adopting the twisted pose of bionics more hindrance than help. Transformed, she slipped from a side door in an unassuming block and joined the crowds. She had gone less than three kilometres before she became aware of the servo-skull following her some metres behind. Yendl was too well practised to reveal she had noticed. She picked up speed. The skull did likewise, a constant presence amid the confusing whirl of aerial constructs going about their duty.

She selected an ambush site. A one-man lift ascended to a gallery hanging from the lower floors of a kilometre-long hab complex. A covered walkway led off into the building there. She ascended the lift, and went down the alley. Sure enough, the skull followed. A junction beckoned, and she took an abrupt left.

When the skull came, she was waiting with her cloak, whirling it out like a net and catching the device mid-flight. She hauled it to earth, her strength overcoming its anti-gravity field and bouncing it from the floor. She wrestled it into submission, and freed it from the cloak. A standard model, bronze-plated ancient bone, long tendrils of interface cabling hanging from its rear. By the standards of Mars, wholly unremarkable, and unarmed. It stopped struggling.

'Message, message, message,' gargled the skull, its glass eyes flashing.

'Speak,' said Yendl.

A click sounded as a vox-feed engaged. 'I have been searching for you everywhere.'

'My well-placed friend.'

'The very same,' said Urquidex. He sounded agitated.

'I hope for your sake this feed is encrypted.'

'Of course!' he snapped. 'But we must be brief. The privacy of this channel cannot be guaranteed for long. One of your colleagues has met with an unfortunate end and the secrecy of your cell is compromised. It will take the diagnostic covens a little time to retrieve the information from the cortex – organics are so much less forgiving than mechanisms – but they will.'

'She is dead? I had guessed,' said Yendl.

'Yes. I am sorry.'

'Sorrow helps nobody.'

'I have other news,' said Urquidex. 'The Fabricator General has embarked on new work. I do not know what. I am attempting to find out.'

'Orks,' said Yendl.

'What?'

'Thousands of ork corpses are being delivered–'

'To the laboratoria of Pavonis Mons?'

'Yes,' said Yendl. 'I have come from there. I was seen.'

'Disaster!' said Urquidex.

Yendl let the servo-skull free. It bobbed level with her eyes.

'Tell me something I am unaware of,' she said. 'Tell me what they want with so many dead orks.'

'I do not know,' said Urquidex. 'Kubik told me himself, Magos Van Auken heads a work as important as the Grand Experiment.' He paused. 'I delay all I can, but cannot do so indefinitely. I cannot stop the Grand Experiment.' A faint crackle sounded on the connection. 'Danger comes. I must go. Stay alive. I will attempt contact soon.'

The skull flew away, becoming one among hundreds hurrying through the tunnel. Yendl lost sight of it quickly. She was not so naive as to believe she could disappear so easily.

FIFTEEN

Lord Guilliman's decree

The day after the attack on the ork moon, the Space Marines of the Last Wall prepared to receive Lord Guilliman Udin Macht Udo with as much ceremony and pomp as if he had in truth been the primarch himself.

They waited on the embarkation deck of the *Abhorrence* in full wargear. Udo's magnificently decorated shuttle pierced the integrity field of the portal majoris and came in to land upon the golden aquila painted specially for the purpose at the centre of the deck. The landing ramp descended, disgorging fifty Lucifer Blacks in gleaming wargear. They jogged down an avenue of Space Marines made up from members of every company of every Chapter in the Last Wall. Fists Exemplar stood with Black Templars beside Iron Knights. Crimson Fists waited proudly alongside Excoriators. With these representatives of each Chapter, there were nigh-on one thousand Space Marines present on the deck.

At the end of this aisle lined by ceramite stood the

GUY HALEY

commanders of the Chapters: the captains and Chaplains of every company, headed by their leaders High Marshal Bohemond of the Black Templars, Chapter Master Issachar of the Excoriators, Chapter Master Quesadra of the Crimson Fists, Chapter Master Thane of the Fists Exemplar, First Captain Verpall of the Iron Knights, and Koorland, Chapter Master and last member of the Imperial Fists.

The Lucifer Blacks stamped shining boots in thunderous march down the ranks of Space Marines. They spread themselves out along the length of the way from Udo's ship to the Chapter Masters until they formed a cordon one man wide. Then they rotated ninety degrees to face into the avenue, their final stamp echoing away into the empty spaces of the embarkation deck. For all the Lucifer Blacks' stern martial polish, there was something faintly ridiculous about this show of defence, as if all of them together could possibly hope to halt even ten of the transhuman warriors, should they decide to kill the Lord Guilliman.

Koorland pushed the implied insult to the back of his mind. More politics. Udo was making a show of his authority.

To a fanfare of silver clarions, Udin Macht Udo came down the ramp of his ship, surrounded by attendants and high-ranking officials of the Adeptus Terra. The train of his cloak was held from the ground by six blind auto-praisers whispering ceaseless prayers to the Emperor. Udo wore all the panoply of his office, a rich uniform stiff with brocade and frogging, a chest full of honours and medallions. Servo-skulls buzzed out in a cloud over his entourage, and swooped off in every direction. Cyber-cherubs came after, four spreading out to hold a cloth of gold two metres over the Lord Guilliman, two more swinging censers which billowed oily blue, perfumed smoke.

This parade came to a halt before the Chapter Masters. The sons of Dorn got down on one knee, and bowed their heads.

Udo clapped his hands and smiled.

'Rise, rise, loyal servants of the Imperium! You, the mighty sons of the Emperor, return to your Father in the time of need, and you have not disappointed Him.'

The Space Marines got to their feet, dwarfing the Lord Guilliman. Unperturbed, Udo motioned for a cybernetic servant bearing a velvet-covered tray, on which were arrayed multiple honour badges. A hooded adept came after, and began to clamp the badges to the Chapter Masters' armour. 'In recognition, this mark is designated the Defence of Terra. You shall be permitted to display it upon your armours and banners for evermore.'

The adept approached Koorland gingerly. With unsteady hands he placed the award upon the bottom corner of his pauldron. The man was shaking with fear. Koorland looked over the head of the adept at the crowd of servants behind Udo. There were four auto-scribes, quill arms scratching down an account of the event upon spools of paper spilling from chest boxes. There were others making records – servitors with pict-capture units for eyes and vox-thieves for mouths. Several of the servo-skulls hovered in place, glass eye-lenses fixed on the Space Marines. They watched also, doubtless capturing the ceremony from other angles.

Another way to show power, thought Koorland. He comes aboard our ships, a statement of ownership. He wondered

how many times these images would be displayed on the pict screens of the Palace, in places like the Fields of Winged Victory, in the innumerable squares and plazas of Terra. How many times the news-criers would shout out Udo's generosity, how many priests would read of how the lords of six Space Marine Chapters demonstrated their allegiance to Terra on their knees before Udin Macht Udo.

'And now, brave defenders of the Imperium,' Udo said, holding his hands high in seeming blessing. 'We must convene a council of war. The ork is not yet defeated.'

A projection of Terra rotated lazily over a chart desk set into the middle of the strategium table, the ork moon its unwelcome companion. Through a long galleried window the same scene could be seen in reality. The gathered might of five Chapters sailed in tight formation around the moon. Wings of interdiction fighters shone bright as polished badges as they swooped over it, their numbers and flight paths reproduced as graphical ideograms over the light image.

The Chapter Masters sat around the massive table. Udin Macht Udo occupied a tall throne at its head, built up so that he might look the Space Marines in the eye. Behind him a broad-winged bronze aquila glowered down from the wall, its one-eyed glare mirroring Udo's own.

'Those vessels taken from the Merchant Fleets that we could not retake, we have destroyed,' Quesadra was saying. 'Our combined forces inflicted significant damage throughout the moon. Our estimates are that two-thirds or more of the orks were killed. The outer surface has been stripped of weaponry. For the time being, the moon poses no significant threat. Chapter Master Koorland's expedition into the moon's core damaged a device that proved to be a long-range teleport array. Without it, the orks cannot reinforce themselves. They are cut off. This intelligence is of the highest significance for the prosecution of the war. The moon–'

'The moon is not only an attack vessel, but a form of spatial gateway. I was informed by Fabricator General Kubik this morning,' said Udo dismissively. 'It has been noted. New strategies are being formulated. The question for now is, was it permanently disabled?'

'We do not think so,' said Thane. 'The power supply was severely damaged, but deep auspex scans show continued power fluctuations. The possibility remains that they may repair it.'

'And then the problem will be as it was before, hundreds of thousands of orks moving in to directly attack Terra,' said Issachar. 'The capabilities of the gateway are unknown. They may be able to bring in replacement materiel and ships. The throneworld remains vulnerable.'

'There remains only one solution,' said Koorland. 'We must attack again.'

An aide handed Udo a data-slate. He squinted at it a while, leaving the Chapter Masters to wait, then handed it back.

'No,' he said forcefully. 'Second Captain Koorland of the Daylight Wall Company, you will not attack again. Not yet.'

'We will leave it there?' said Bohemond incredulously. 'The Last Wall has been called! We come to Terra's aid, and you would deny the Emperor this victory?'

'Lord Bohemond,' said Koorland. 'Please. Hear the Lord Guilliman out.'

'Listen to the second captain, he has some wisdom,' said Udo.

Issachar's face darkened. 'Koorland is a Chapter Master of the Adeptus Astartes, Lord Guilliman,' he said. 'He sits here with us in brotherhood. It pains me to remind one of your exalted rank.'

'I do not require your assistance,' said Udo. 'Koorland is no Chapter Master. By the customs of his own order, if not directly nominated by the passing commander, potential successors to the office of Chapter Master of the Imperial Fists must be selected by the consensus of the Chapter's Chaplains and wall captains, and those favoured with nomination voted for. In Koorland's case neither of these criteria have been met.'

'How could they be? He is the only one,' growled Bohemond. 'The last Imperial Fist.'

'Would the same stand if he were the last surviving neophyte?' said Udo. 'I think not.'

'He has been recognised as Chapter Master by us, the lords of the other sons of Dorn,' said Issachar. 'He has led us in battle. He is worthy.'

Udo spread his hands, neither dismissing or conceding the point. 'Far be it from me to deny the will of so many mighty heroes. Terra could conceivably allow such a selection, if it proved to be in the best interests of the Imperium.'

'The affairs of the Adeptus Astartes are our own!' said Bohemond.

'But they are not, High Marshal,' said Udo patiently. 'They

are yours as far as any of the other adepta's. You are, first and foremost, servants and subjects of the God-Emperor, Lord of all Mankind – a species of which, although your alterations perhaps stretch the classification, you are still a member, High Marshal. Your Chapter forgets this fact a little too often. Your fleets are unaccountable, rumours persist of an excess of warriors under your command, and your actions have stirred up previously quiet xenos races too many times.'

'We serve the Emperor,' said Bohemond, 'not bureaucrats. Ours is a sacred mission.'

'We are the agents of the Emperor's will,' countered Udo. 'Not some officio to be ignored.' He lowered his voice. 'Your wilfulness gives us pause. This gathering of yours was neither called for nor authorised. Now we have three thousand Space Marines in orbit over the Golden Throne itself. What are we to make of that?'

'In the face of your incompetence we save the throneworld, and you come to accuse us of treachery?' said Quesadra in disgust.

'You are the largest force of Space Marines assembled since the Heresy,' said Udo. 'We must be left in no doubt as to where your allegiances lie. Your success is welcome, and applauded. But your unannounced arrival here in such strength has the Senatorum Imperialis in uproar.'

'If the Senatorum had proved a little more effective in governing, and a little less in pursuing the interests of the senators, then we would not need to be here at all, and my brothers might yet live,' said Koorland quietly.

Udo pulled a face. 'You see, it is words of that sort that fan the flames of my fears. Is that a threat, second captain?'

'We have no interest in usurping the Senatorum!' said Koorland. He rose from his seat. Issachar grabbed his wrist, but Koorland pulled free. He leaned over the table. 'Is this why we were left alone to die upon Ardamantua, because you are afraid of us? Did you expend the lives of the Imperium's staunchest defenders in political calculation?'

'I doubt much thought went into it at all, brother,' said Verpall. 'That is the root of the problem here.'

'Yours is a simple breed,' said Udo. 'Bred for war. You think on nothing but matters of combat and honour. I have seen contempt for the common man too many times in the face of a Space Marine. You think yourselves intelligent, and you are, but you forget too often you are made for conflict, and conflict invariably follows in your wake. Leave the subtleties of government to those better suited, as the Emperor intended.'

'My lord Malfons died to preserve your office,' said Verpall. 'Do not insult us again.'

'There, you see. A veiled threat. Another statement that forges my opinion the harder. You must listen to me. Do as I say and we shall have no difficulty between us. Tomorrow, we will proceed to the surface where you will be feted as the saviours that you are. Then, in the Senatorum Imperialis, you will renew your oaths of fealty to the Imperium. Then you shall be acknowledged as the Chapter Master of the Imperial Fists, Second Captain Koorland, with the full will of the Senatorum. After which, we shall formulate plans – with the backing of myself, the Lord Commander Militant, Lord High Admiral Lansung and the others – to end this crisis.'

The Chapter Masters looked to one another. Quesadra drummed three crimson fingers on the table, *click click click*.

'What of the moon?' asked Koorland.

'Kubik desires it to be left intact.'

'So Terra dances to Mars' tune now?' said Bohemond.

Udo gave him a hard stare. Bohemond returned it. 'We have convened a meeting of the High Twelve,' said Udo. 'There its fate will be decided.'

'I urge you, my lord, it must be destroyed,' said Koorland.

'Whether or not it will be is a matter for the Lords of Terra. You will maintain your blockade until the Navy gathers in sufficient force to take your place. If you perform this task, none shall set foot upon the moon. The Fabricator General has agreed to withdraw his armies for the time being. The moon is under your custodianship. Beyond that it is no longer your concern,' said Udo evenly. 'You have pulled the orks' teeth. Bravo. It is time to let the organs of government decide the best course of action. Know this, lord Chapter Masters, this fleet of yours cannot be allowed to remain whole. Your Chapters shall each receive individual orders. With your might properly directed, we shall end the threat of this Beast once and for all. There shall be no more need for such,' he lifted a hand, 'charming displays of confraternity.'

The Space Marines shifted uneasily.

'Yes, my lord,' said Koorland hesitantly. 'When you order its destruction, we shall be on hand to aid you in your task.'

'There is one last item I must inform you of,' continued Udo. 'We cannot allow the news of the destruction of the Imperial Fists to be made public. Your return, Koorland, will be the proof of the indomitability of the Adeptus Astartes of Dorn's line. You shall return from the dead to great fanfare, the orks cannot defeat you and so forth. I shall have a suitable story provided. You are only one, and that presents a problem. To circumvent this, each of you will provide from among your number Wall Guardians to man the Palace as the Imperial Fists always have.'

'They are not Imperial Fists,' said Quesadra.

'They shall be dressed in the livery of the Imperial Fists,' said Udo. 'The populace shall know no different.'

'Our men will never give up their colours!' exclaimed Issachar.

'There will be no honour? No mention of my brothers' sacrifice?' Koorland's face went pale. 'This is an outrage!'

'This is politics, captain,' said Udo. 'In the aftermath of the moon's arrival, to inform the people that the Imperial Fists are nigh-on extinct will send a wave of terror throughout the Imperium. Worse would be rumours, for they are pernicious and far harder to deal with than the shock of an announcement. Not a single word of this disaster must become public. You have my sympathy for your loss, captain, but there are practicalities to consider.' Udo stood, holding up his hands to forestall disagreement. 'You must forgive me. I return to the surface now. I have much to arrange.'

The Lord Commander bowed sharply, leaving the Space Marines to stare after him as his aides and constructs filed out in his wake.

'We will not break the fleet,' said Bohemond.

'We cannot defy him,' said Quesadra.

'We can,' said Verpall. 'How can Udo possibly enforce the

order? If we did refuse he could do nothing. He would be forced to back down and concoct some story that cast him in a favourable light.'

'More politics,' spat Bohemond.

'I cannot condone that course of action,' said Koorland. 'It is close to heresy.'

'We have no choice,' said Issachar, 'if we are to save the Imperium.'

'A sentiment that has been voiced before,' said Koorland. 'Be careful of your thoughts, brother.'

SIXTEEN

The welcoming of heroes

The Praetorian Way resounded to cheers as the Space Marines marched from the East Gate Landing Hall towards the centre of the Imperial Palace: over three thousand of them, more than had been on Terra at one time for hundreds of years. Millions of citizens lined the route, waving flags bearing the badges of the Chapters. They roared and screamed their approbation, ecstatic at the sight of so many of the Angels of Death. The attack moon loured at them, its porcine face expressing a fury it was impotent to act upon. Aircraft shrieked overhead, pumping coloured smoke into the hazy atmosphere. Laud hailers sang out hymnals and prayers, and servo-skulls bearing vox-projectors roared out the names of the most distinguished battle-brothers, while others recited the Chapter histories of the Space Marines.

Giant screens along the route showed picts of dead orks and burning ships, intercut with the faces of Koorland and his fellow lords, their names and honours written in bold text beneath their images. Music blasted from a hundred

places, until the words and melodies were unrecognisable as coherent sounds; they were sonic fragments, an over-whelming cacophony that outsang the loudest battle.

Never had Koorland heard a million voices scream as one, either in adulation or in pain. He went bareheaded at the High Lords' request, crowned with a laurel wreath. Let the people see their saviour, they said. He envied the twenty sham Imperial Fists marching behind him, their helms locked in place, their audio dampers working at max-imum capacity. Koorland kept his face forward. So many people, so many faces, all of them calling his name. Scented flakes of paper rained down on them from every side. It was intoxicating, and it should not be so. He had performed his duty, that was all. He would not allow himself to indulge his emotions. He would not allow himself the folly of pride.

They passed from tightly clustered buildings and into the killing field before the Palace walls. Four kilometres of bare rock, open to the sky. Daylight Wall dominated it, tinted a delicate rose by the rising sun. The Praetorian Way meekly burrowed its way through the East Gate, little more than a wormhole in the fabric of the wall in comparison to the defence's massive size. The wall was stupefyingly tall. Here Koorland's gene-seed ancestors had fought and died, protecting the Emperor from the gravest enemy of all. What he and his fellow Chapter Masters had accom-plished was nothing by comparison. He reminded himself repeatedly of his own insignificance as they approached the soaring buttresses, towers, gun emplacements and gigantic statuary.

The crowds in the killing field were no less vocal, but free of the resonating plascrete canyons of the outer district the noise was bearable. Daylight Wall, in many senses *his* wall. Koorland had not seen it for so long. The East Gate reared up, mighty now he was before it, its revealed scale making the wall all the more titanic. The reflected heat of the early sun bounced from it, glinting from the polished armour of the Space Marine column. Koorland's wargear gleamed newly. Not even his intention to keep his battle damage on show until his brothers were avenged had survived Udo's blunt realpolitik. Issachar's Chapter were the battered exception, their creed demanding they mark their wounds well.

Koorland marched towards the gate where the multi-lane Praetorian Way became a straight tunnel through the wall. To be coming home like this, alone, the bearer of half-truths and propagandic distortions, blunted the glory of their triumph over the orks. The moon was still in the sky. The wall stood strong in the face of its aggression, but scarring from its attacks opened up gaps all over the Palace's skylines. Despite these reminders of vulnerability around them, the Senatorum Imperialis would doubtless go back to its infighting.

The blackness of the gate tunnel swallowed him, and the crowd's jubilation was silenced. Shame dogged his footsteps and determination drove him on.

This state of affairs could not be allowed to persist. It was a thought that would not be quieted all the way through the giving of honours and renewal of fealty that took place in the Senatorum Imperialis at the end of their march.

* * *

After the ceremony was over, the highest of the high were ushered into a giant hall clad in ornately carved tiles of malachite and onyx. There an interminable feast began, bookended by pompous speeches. The food was quite exquisite, but Koorland was so invested in his problems he found himself insensible to the flavour. He filled himself as he had been trained to long ago, shovelling delicacies into his mouth to fuel his transhuman metabolism as if they were the lowest gruel. There were so many ingredients in each dish that a confusing amount of information flooded his brain via his neuroglottis, further darkening his mood.

After the feast came the reception, a grand and tedious party where Koorland was besieged by a stream of dignitaries that would not stop flowing. Their mouths dripped honeyed comments, a request or criticism behind every one. Koorland politely listened to his interlocutors, insisting he had no say in the policies of the Senatorum Imperialis, and that he had no intention of parlaying the assembled Chapters' might into political influence. 'I am a servant of the Emperor,' and its variations became a phrase repeated as often as a battle catechism.

The High Twelve and many of the greatest of the lesser lords kept themselves distant from him. Those that attempted an approach shied away under Udo's glowering. When Vangorich appeared at his side it was so unexpected that Koorland did not at first recognise him.

'Good evening, Chapter Master,' said a wiry man. He surveyed the room, not lifting his face to look at the Imperial Fist. Koorland prepared himself for the usual back and forth of insincere small talk and relentless probing, but something made him hesitate in returning the man's greeting. He was armed only with a goblet of wine and a sardonic manner, but there was something about him, a mixture of poise, alertness and confidence that the others lacked and that signalled he was the most dangerous man in the room. Then he looked up, held out a hand, and Koorland knew him.

'Drakan Vangorich,' said Koorland.

Koorland's giant fist engulfed Vangorich's hand and they shook in the civilian manner, palm to palm.

'I recognise you from our discussion. I thank you for your... recent good wishes.'

'I am only happy they were well received,' said Vangorich.

'How could I not heed you? You are dangerous,' said Koorland.

'My, you are blunt. You don't think these other fine ladies and gentlemen are?' said Vangorich.

'Not in the same way as you,' said Koorland. 'Not immediately. None of them would stand a chance against me in combat, but I suspect you might. And you also possess their political power. There are several of the greatest lords of the Space Marines in this chamber, but I think you are the most dangerous of us all.'

Vangorich shrugged slightly. He was small by unaltered human standards, and minute by those of the transhumans.

'Correct again, Chapter Master. I suppose I am exceptionally dangerous. Shall I tell you another difference between myself and my fellow High Lords? You and I, Koorland, are on the same side.'

'We are all on the same side,' said Koorland. 'The orks are on the other.'

'Oh, Chapter Master, please!' Vangorich tutted. Koorland noticed that when the Assassin spoke he hid his lips from prying eyes behind his goblet. 'Don't play the naïf with me. I'm a remarkably good judge of a man's mood no matter their type. A necessary skill in my role. It is plain that you are not pleased nor are you satisfied by what you see here on Terra.'

'I am not,' admitted Koorland. 'My brothers are all dead. I hold the men and women in this hall responsible.'

'You are not alone in doing so. There are others of us who are frustrated by the failure of the Senatorum to contain the orks. Now that, Chapter Master, is why we are on the same side. I am sorry, by the way, about your brothers. There was one, Daylight, who was a passing acquaintance of mine.'

Koorland looked down at Vangorich hard. Daylight had been his company representative on Terra. 'I have had enough of barbed words hidden in flattery. If you seek to goad me, I advise you to seek your sport elsewhere.'

'I mean nothing ill by it,' said Vangorich. 'I will not say Daylight was my friend, but I spoke with him every day and I always regarded him well. He was an honourable man. It is a shame he realised his dream of going to war. It proved his end.'

'War is our purpose. To die in battle is an honour.' As Koorland said the words he doubted them. He remembered the devastation on Ardamantua. There had been little honour won there.

'How refreshing,' said Vangorich. 'These others here, some few of them might hold such noble sentiments. Juskina Tull,' he pointed out a tall woman in a complicated dress. She held herself aloof, and her face was blank of emotion. 'She, for example, for all her delusions in initiating the Proletarian Crusade, her motives were at least pure – in part. Many of the rest of them cannot even claim that. They do not see beyond their own concerns, or they actively promote their own interests. Naturally, they all invoke the Emperor, and the good of the Imperium. But frankly it never ceases to amaze me how convenient it is that the will of the Emperor coincides with the aims of every High Lord, no matter how contradictory their statements appear when set one beside another.

'See,' said Vangorich, pointing. 'The Provost, Zeck. He is perhaps a little overly concerned with his office. He is very good at his job, but too good to be effective on the council. Lord Commander Militant Verreault is at odds with Lord High Admiral Lansung, and is in Udo's pocket. The telepaths Anwar and Sark are occupied so much with their own, vital efforts to keep the Imperium together that they are too easily swayed by quick solutions, whereas the Paternoval Envoy Gibran cannot be swayed at all.' As he spoke, he indicated the High Lords one at a time. 'Lansung is a brilliant military commander, but of all of them he is the most responsible for this sorry mess.'

'His ship stood back while we attacked,' said Koorland.

'As it did when Tull's Crusade went forward. I cannot think why. He has perhaps lost his self-belief. I'm sure his own follies were driven by the idea that he was the best man for the job. That only he knows the way to extend the Imperium's reach. But his manoeuvring was nearly the end of us. They all think that they alone know the answer. Confidence and zealotry, a terrible mix. He hoarded his fleet when he should have attacked, all for the chance at an office he will now never hold. The Inquisition seeks to repair the machineries of government, but cannot agree with itself and falls to infighting.

'The fat man there in three countesses' worth of jewellery is Mesring, the Ecclesiarch. A less holy man I have rarely met. And let us not forget Kubik, of course, hiding away on Mars up to no good. He's turning into something of a threat to the Imperium, between you and me. All the signs suggest he seeks to assert the supremacy of Mars over that of Terra.' He sighed and waved his goblet around him, taking in all the dignitaries, toadies, servers, servitors and every other human being in the room. 'A room full of agendas does not make for happy governance. It is, all things told, a sorry mess of a game.'

'I cannot see this as a game, Grand Master.'

'But it is a game, Koorland,' said Vangorich. 'A very serious game, but a game nonetheless.'

'If all the pieces are compromised, then what is left?' said Koorland.

'What is left is you and I,' said Vangorich, tapping a finger against Koorland's chest eagle. 'So we best hope you are successful in hauling our collective skins out of the fire. I do not wish to see the time come when the Imperium has to rely on the Grand Master of the Assassinorum. We are gardeners, we Assassins. A snip and a prune. We are not intended for the wholesale remodelling of government, or, the Emperor forfend, the wielding of power.' He smiled innocently, his scar twisting his face. Unlike Udo's disfigurement, it somehow made the Assassin appear even more genial.

For a man who protested his lack of interest in power, thought Koorland, he seemed remarkably adept at wielding it.

'Ah, my goblet appears to be empty,' said Vangorich. 'This evening, I feel like drinking. This week has been taxing.' He rested a hand on Koorland's vambrace, and said sotto voce, 'Let us continue this some other time.' Vangorich sauntered off, greeting men and women with a warmth shot through with insolence.

Thane came to his side. The Chapter Masters had been besieged by coteries of adepts, some of whom were there at Udo's behest to keep them apart. But when a Space Marine in full battleplate chose to move through a room, people had no choice but to quickly remove themselves from his path.

'I tire of their flattery and wheedling,' said Thane.

'This room is a vipers' nest,' said Koorland.

'Aye, and Grand Master Vangorich is the biggest snake of all. Be wary of him, brother.'

'A life of war, of bolt and blade, was preferable to this,' said Koorland.

'I agree. But Issachar has it right. We have a different kind of battle to fight now.' The supplicants kept their distance from the Chapter Masters' quiet conference, all save one: the fat man sealed into ceremonial ecclesiarchal robes so encrusted in jewels they were thick as battleplate, Ecclesiarch Mesring. He came over, sweating under the weight of his robes of office despite the four hollow-eyed, shaven-headed acolytes holding his train. A whole host of others trailed him: priests, scribes, and petitioners anxiously awaiting a moment to speak with him.

Mesring interrupted the Space Marines impolitely. 'Chapter Masters! I come to offer my thanks. You do the Emperor's duty. He is pleased.'

Koorland turned from his conversation with Thane. 'You are Mesring, Ecclesiarch of the Adeptus Ministorum?'

Mesring was taken aback at Koorland's feigned ignorance, but rallied well. 'A grandiose title for a humble role. I am fortunate to interpret the Emperor's will.' He bowed stiffly from the waist, his chins wobbling with the effort. 'And it is glorious to stand before His favoured servants, His holy sons.' His pale flesh gleamed, and he slurred his words despite his manners. Koorland suspected he was drunk.

'Your garb tells another story than humility,' said Thane. 'You tell me the Emperor is pleased? Who are you to know?'

'You gainsay the will of the Holy Emperor?' said Mesring.

'Your religion means nothing to me,' said Thane. 'My Chapter follows the tenets of the Imperial Truth, set down by the Emperor during the Great Crusade. How quickly you have forgotten it. We are not holy. Do not treat us as such.'

'One thousand five hundred years is a long time, Chapter Master,' said Mesring. 'The Imperial Truth is all but forgotten. The scriptures tell us that the Emperor conceived of it as a necessary lie. The very name is an exercise in irony. Only in death has the Emperor cast off His corporeal cloak and revealed Himself to us in His true glory!'

'I disagree,' said Thane. 'Your cult profanes His memory with idolatry.'

'When will the Adeptus Astartes see the light?' said

Mesring. 'It troubles me, my son, that the Emperor's own angels deny the truth.'

'We are not angels!' snorted Thane.

'You were among those who urged the populace to take the oath of crusade?' said Koorland.

'I did, I did! As was only right.'

'It proved to be wholly wrong,' said Koorland. 'A rash move that risked provoking the orks, and cost the lives of millions, while you and Tull and the others who promoted it remain alive and well.'

A flicker of consternation crossed Mesring's face. 'Then it is good that you are here now, to fight them on our behalf.'

'Aye, that is what we are, priest – warriors,' said Thane.

'One day, I hope to bring all our mighty warriors into the truth of the faith. Some are perhaps more amenable than others.' His gaze strayed around the room, looking for someone. He smiled secretly to himself.

'Then go and speak to them,' said Thane. He glared menacingly at Mesring until the Ecclesiarch made his excuses and left.

A surge of anger built in Koorland's chest. The men and women around him had been scheming while Terra burned. The temptation to sweep it all aside was great.

'I am done here,' he told Thane. 'I return to the fleet. The Senatorum is broken, all the High Lords invested only in their own advancement. I have heard the name of the Emperor invoked by every charlatan in this house. This cannot be allowed to continue.'

With that he departed the room, the crowd parting hurriedly before him.

SEVENTEEN

War in the dust

Magneric stamped over the gritty ruin of Dzelenic IV, assault cannon blazing. Orks filled the surface from horizon to horizon. More came thundering down from orbit in rickety landing craft, little more than balls of scrap that bounced to a halt on the ground before bursting into pieces. Sometimes they fell apart to reveal their mangled occupants, but more often than not mobs of howling greenskins came running out, shooting their weapons into the air. Magneric ploughed through them unconcerned, killing them without thought, the eye of his Dreadnought fixed upon the low ruin the Iron Warriors had occupied, visible over the ridge of a dune. By the gunfire flashing out, Kalkator still lived.

The ammunition counters in Magneric's display blinked to orange as his assault cannon ran to below half capacity. The view Magneric had of the outside world was grainy, bleached out, striped with the lines of inferior pict capture. Reticules danced over his view, highlighting targets of

priority, data-screeds and numerical data further crowding his vision, but he saw well enough to kill.

His flesh body floated in the sarcophagus at the machine's heart. He was dimly aware of it, the hurts that it still suffered, the limbs that it lacked. It did not trouble him. Others given the singular honour of internment spoke of disassociation, a feeling of distance from the world of the living and a weariness that became harder and harder to bear. Magneric did not feel this. He considered the metal behemoth he dwelled within as his own flesh and blood, an extension of his will. Magneric refused to sleep like the others, and retained his rank and his own name, for Magneric had hatred to drive him onward. Kalkator was the wellspring and the object of this fury, an emotion pure in its heat and ferocity. Magneric lived for Kalkator's death.

'Kalkator! Kalkator! I will come and end you!' He caught an ork in his power fist and crushed it flat, hurling the gory remains back into its fellows and bowling them over. Those that got back up again he gunned down with a spray of fire from his storm bolter.

'The Emperor has decreed that I slay you, traitor! I am coming for you!'

Magneric was the ebon spear point of an unstoppable blade. His warriors came in his wake, driving through the orkish attack. Behind him Chaplain Aladucos chanted hymnals in praise of the Emperor, encouraging Magneric's warriors to greater acts of violence. The Black Templars gunships duelled with ork fighters overhead. Three lay in smoking ruin four kilometres behind their advance. Magneric's own craft sent a column of black smoke climbing skyward, but it did not matter. Only to go forward, to slaughter the foes of the Emperor, to continue the crusade to conquer the galaxy in the name of mankind!

Death was all that mattered to Magneric.

Let Baldon wheedle at him to rest, let Ralstan admonish him for his lack of maintenance slumber. He would sleep when the stain of Kalkator's existence was wiped from the galaxy.

'Onwards, brothers, in the name of the Emperor! Strike down these animals and carve a path towards those who betrayed the Lord of Terra. Feel His holy wrath. Kill the ork that we might strike down the traitors! Wash the sands of this dead world with their blood, and then let us away, and conquer, conquer, conquer in the Emperor's name!'

Magneric surged on, batting orks from his path, until the rabble thinned and gave out. The crowd was behind him. He shot down the last few orks between him and the dune, gyros shifting within his body to compensate for the slip of the sand. He came over the crest, and looked down at the Iron Warriors' last desperate redoubt.

It had been a building of unguessable height. The top part had been sheared away in the cataclysm that had destroyed the world, leaving sprouts of tangled rebar jutting from crumbling nubs of rockcrete. Three floors alone remained, set in a slight hollow scoured out by the actions of the wind blasting around the building, the bottommost level half-buried in the sand. The ruin had few windows, and one door. Perhaps that lack of apertures was why it had stood a thousand years in the face of howling winds

while others around it had been worn down to angular patterns in the sand. The sole entrance was on the side facing Magneric, choked to the top with windblown dust. He rumbled with satisfaction. The traitors' last Thunderhawk had come down hard a quarter of a kilometre away, ploughing up shattered concrete from the barren fields of the desert. The wreck smoked still. The Iron Warriors were going nowhere.

The glint of steel in the ruddy sunlight revealed Iron Warriors manning the building. A ring of dead orks three deep surrounded it, staining the dust black with their blood. None had come within twenty metres of the position and lived. The building was angled, knocked to one side by seismic upheaval, its rockcrete scoured rough by the dead world's unforgiving weather. Cracks spidered it on all sides. As battered as Kalkator's Great Company, it was nevertheless a serviceable fortress, and the Iron Warriors were far from beaten.

Magneric paused, revelling in the moment before he would crush his foe. Behind him the howl of the orks quietened, and the hard clatter of weapons fire abated. His sergeants, Chaplain and castellan all voxed him reporting the same thing from all fronts: the orks were withdrawing.

Laughing in triumph, Magneric stamped forward, sending crescents of sand skidding out in front of him, to stand at the edge of the killing field.

'Kalkator!' he boomed. 'Kalkator! Come out, come out! You are caught! The orks retreat, and you face only me and my judgement. You are run to earth. Come out from your den and face me not as an animal, but as the noble warrior you once were. Ask for mercy, repent your sins against the Emperor and I shall absolve you of your transgressions with a swift death!'

Silence. Magneric's vox clicked.

'My lord,' said Ralstan. 'The orks have scattered, but I have reports from Ericus that there are many, many more inbound. The *Obsidian Sky* has been unable to engage with the *Palimodes* and is beset on all sides. Further ork craft are approaching. Be quick with this. We must leave!'

A noise of dissatisfaction rumbled from Magneric's vox-emitter. 'Kalkator! Answer me!'

This time a voice sounded from the building in reply. 'Magneric! So high must I be in your regard, that you chase me for a thousand years and more, into the teeth of the greatest ork Waaagh! since Ullanor!'

'Kalkator!' boomed the Dreadnought. His pneumatics hissed, and the great block of his right shoulder shifted, lifting his assault cannon high. The barrels spun once, and halted. Magneric's targeting array danced over the ruin, picking out the Iron Warriors in green outlines. Kalkator was not among them.

'You are looking well. Iron without suits you.'

'I am unmoved by your mockery,' boomed Magneric. 'Come out so that I might kill you!'

Other Black Templars gathered on the dune, kneeling down to take cover behind its ridge. Ralstan directed some of his warriors to fan out to the left and right to surround the building. They were respectfully silent. Kalkator and Magneric were veterans of the Heresy war. To hear them speak was to hear echoes of that awful conflict.

'I ask for parley!' shouted Kalkator.

'You shall have none!' roared Magneric. 'I bring only the mercy of death, not a desire to speak.'

'Then let me rephrase my offer,' said Kalkator. 'Three las-cannons are pointed at your sarcophagus. If you refuse parley, or if you accept it and attempt to kill me, then I will have them open fire and burn whatever sorry scrap of flesh still exists within that machine.'

Silence fell. Evening was coming. The sinking sun, invisible behind its shroud of dust, pushed Magneric's shadow out so that it fell upon Kalkator's redoubt, grey and inflated in the scattered light.

'Our auspexes detect a massive concentration of orks coming towards our position,' said Kalkator. 'Thousands. You are merely seventy-three warriors. You cannot hold them. I am quite content to sit here and watch them butcher you. But there is another way.'

'My lord, he is correct,' said Castellan Ralstan. 'As Ericus informed us, orks are landing in number to the west. What are your orders?'

'Do you hear them coming?' goaded Kalkator.

'My lord!' said Ralstan.

Magneric roared. 'Very well! Parley!'

'Swear upon your honour you will not harm me,' said Kalkator.

'My acceptance of your truce is my bond! An oath is not required,' bellowed Magneric indignantly.

'Nevertheless, say it,' said Kalkator.

'You have my word,' said Magneric proudly.

Kalkator emerged on the roof of the building, standing up

from whatever hiding place he had been skulking in. 'Then let us talk,' he said.

For the first time in centuries, Kalkator stood facing Magneric. Caesax and his vexillary flanked the warsmith, the banner of his Great Company rippling in the cooling wind. Magneric's Sword Brethren made a shallow arc about him, Ralstan at his side. Hatred glared out from eye-lenses set in black and iron-grey armour.

After a moment's thought, Kalkator reached up and unsealed his helm. He lifted it from his head, and looked upon the Dreadnought with unmoderated eyes.

'It is good to see you, Magneric.'

Magneric's sole glass eye stared unblinkingly back. Upon his sensorium feed, reticules locked onto Kalkator's vulnerable points glowed red and screamed that he should destroy the traitor.

'Do not seek to play upon old affections!' he snarled, his vox-emitters expressing his sentiment as an inhuman machine growl.

'We found ourselves on opposite sides of the war,' said Kalkator. 'I do not see why that should invalidate our friendship.'

'You turned on everything we fought for! You betrayed the Imperium, and cast your lot in with the Dark Powers of the universe. You have ruined mankind.'

Kalkator's lip curved. 'We did betray the Emperor, if such you can call abandoning the service of a liar who concealed the truth of reality from those who loved Him, who used our Legion carelessly. You might call it betrayal, freeing mankind from the fetters of oppression, allowing the strong to prevail, showing our kind the real meaning of a power that is accessible to all, not just those self-appointed guardians who hide their purposes behind untruths and oppression.'

'You are the oppressors,' said Magneric. 'Your words are false.'

'The sons of our lowliest slaves might one day join our Legion. And if they are imbued with our iron, then they shall stand strong, knowing fully in their hearts that they serve the most honest masters of all – themselves. It is you who is mistaken, dear Magneric. You Imperial Fists and that braggart father of yours. You are blind to the truth.'

'I am Imperial Fist no longer,' said Magneric, 'but a Black Templar, and I am party to a greater truth. The powers of Old Night have deceived and corrupted you.'

'And what new truth is this, I wonder?' said Kalkator, gesturing at the relics hanging from the Dreadnought, and the texts painted upon his armour.

'Devotion to the only one who might save us all from the hell of the warp. It was always thus.'

'I say you are wrong,' said Kalkator. 'You say I am wrong. We could stand here all day and argue who is right and who is not while the orks come over that dune and hack us into pieces. Let us agree that both of us wish mankind to survive, only that we differ in the method.'

'You are self-serving. Evil. The Emperor offers genuine salvation to the human race.'

'Be that as it may, I do not think the orks are going to listen to your sermonising as long as I have.'

'I will not fight alongside you again, Kalkator.'

'Are you ashamed, Magneric?' said Kalkator. 'Is that why you pursue me so recklessly? I remember a time when our comradeship was lauded as an example of how our Legions could set aside their differences and find brotherhood.'

'A trust and bond you betrayed.'

'I could say the same of you. We fought together, Magneric. We must do so again. The alternatives are poor. We can kill each other now, or let the orks slay us one after the other. Together, we have a chance. Together, we might leave this world.'

'A few hours ago, you might have made your escape. But the orks fill the skies. You lack sufficient flight support to break free,' gloated Magneric. 'Your gunships would never make it to the surface to extract you.'

'Air cover would be part of the price of our cooperation,' said Kalkator. 'We fight together, we leave together. You allow us to depart the system, and then if you really must you can continue this wasteful pursuit for another thousand years.'

Ralstan voxed the Dreadnought privately. 'As much as I hate to say this, my lord, the warsmith does have a point. Together our numbers are doubled. Nearly one hundred and fifty Space Marines against the orks, we will prevail.'

'They no longer have the right to name themselves Legiones Astartes!' roared Magneric for all to hear. He stamped from one foot to the other. 'They are traitors, nothing more!'

'We are Space Marines, Magneric,' said Kalkator. 'Deny it all you will, but the same gifts your warriors possess are ours too. We must fight together, or we will all perish.'

'Never!'

'Think how much more good you will be able to do if you survive to continue your foolish crusades. How many xenos will live if you die, how many human worlds will call out for protection from the predation of mankind's foes and you will not be there to answer? Neither of us want mankind to fall. Today we have a common enemy. Communicate your agreement with the *Obsidian Sky*, and I shall command the *Palimodes* to fight alongside your ship. If they do not stand united, your craft will never make it to the surface either. Do not be a fool, Magneric. Remember our battles, and how often I was right then. I am right now.'

A long moment passed. No words were forthcoming. The two lines of Space Marines faced each other silently.

Kalkator shook his head, and replaced his helm. 'You are making a grave mistake. I will return to my warriors, and we shall–'

'Wait!' said Magneric, his voice low and distorted, the aged vox-equipment popping. 'I reluctantly agree. We will fight side by side, one more time. Hear me, warriors of the Black Templars!' He rotated from side to side, addressing all his followers. 'No member of our Chapter is to harm the Iron Warriors until our treaty is sundered. So swear I, Magneric, Marshal of the Kalkator Crusade. Ralstan, command Ericus to aid the Iron Warriors ship. Have him provide me an estimated extraction time.' Magneric bent down, his sarcophagus slit glowing in the failing light. 'We will leave this world together, Kalkator, or not at all. Do not think to betray me.'

'You have my word that I will abide by the terms of our

agreement,' said Kalkator, 'more for the sake of our old friendship than for anything else. Now come! Bring your warriors into the redoubt. We must make our preparations.'

EIGHTEEN

Red Haven minus one, plus one

Water, so rare a commodity on arid Mars, ran wastefully from a loose pipe connector. Orange slime furred the join, a mix of rust and biological contamination that hung half a metre down the wall. The water ran down this trailing, slimy beard, dripping silently into a slick puddle more algae than moisture. This patch of errant water was the only distinguishing feature of the pressure-release chamber Yendl waited in. Rust streaked the walls. A dead servo-skull, perhaps the drone that was supposed to report on damage like the leak, lay dusty in the corner. No sign of water flooding was apparent; evidently no pressure release had been needed in this part of the system for a long time. It was unremarkable, overlooked. The ideal place for the cadre to meet.

Yendl was tense but calm. The sense of imminent discovery had lessened. She had a new identity, assumed at the cost of another's life. The orange robes of a mid-ranking data-tech cloaked her stooped body, her limbs twisted into a new shape. Even waiting for her fellows she maintained the disguise.

Yendl blinked. Mariazet Isolde was suddenly there in the round door drain at the base of the chamber ramp. Her face was new, polymorphine-warped, but in the company of Yendl she did not keep up the rest of her pretence. She moved as an Assassin, without sound, every footstep deliberate, her body the acme of poise. She joined Yendl. They did not speak. Haast was the last member of Red Haven to come.

'You are tardy,' said Isolde.

'I was followed,' said Haast.

'Did you lose them?' asked Yendl.

'Better than that,' said Haast. 'Wait.'

She disappeared for little over a minute, then returned carrying a man, gagged and bound hand and foot, over her shoulder. He was larger than her, but she bore him easily. Haast dropped him on the rockcrete. Hard.

'He's been trailing me a week now. I decided it was time to find out who he is.'

'Verraux is dead,' said Yendl. Haast nodded, her eyes fixed on her prisoner.

'That I suspected,' said Isolde. 'I have had no word from her for some time.'

'I was nearly discovered,' said Yendl.

'Are we further compromised?' asked Isolde.

'They look for me, but cannot find me,' said Yendl. 'My information gathering suffers – I must find new access to the Martian noosphere. They are watching the old ways.'

'That is acceptable,' said Isolde. 'Tybalt?'

'He is hidden still,' said Haast. 'I moved his cryo-pod a

week ago and checked on it before coming here. No signs of detection.'

'Then matters could be worse,' said Isolde. 'Let us deal with this one while we wait for the message.'

Haast bent to the man's head and ripped his gag free. He looked at the three Assassins confidently.

'We work to the same goals,' he said without preamble. 'I mean you no harm. You can release me.'

'We will be the judges of that,' said Yendl. 'Who are you, who do you work for?'

'Whoever I'm told to be, but I've been ordered to reveal my purpose should my life be threatened by you.'

'I'd say it is threatened,' said Isolde, her hand straying to her knife.

'I can only agree,' said the man.

Isolde squatted down next to him. 'Your name is Raznick. You work for Wienand.'

'Now how did you come by that information?' said Raznick.

Isolde tapped her head. 'Memcore implant. I have a record of every Inquisitorial agent active in the Sol System.'

'The ones you know about,' said Raznick.

'I know about you,' said Isolde.

'Wienand's dead,' said Haast. 'You're out of a job.'

'Is she now?' said Raznick.

'What is your mission?' asked Yendl.

'Observation, nothing more. I was told to keep an eye on you, make sure Lord Vangorich doesn't have you do anything rash.'

Isolde scowled. 'You of the Inquisition, the keepers of the Imperium. Amateurs.'

'Maybe I wanted to get caught?' said Raznick.

'Right,' said Isolde. 'Because you want me to make a hole in your brain. Clever.'

'Shh!' hissed Haast.

Suddenly, all three members of the Assassinorum cell had pistols in their hands and trained on the drainage door. A faint skittering came up the enclosed canal outside. Isolde moved to the bottom of the ramp. They waited as the pattering grew louder.

A rat appeared in the door, weirdly long-limbed and long-bodied, a Terran animal adapted to the lower-gravity conditions of Mars.

'It is here,' said Isolde, holstering her weapon. The rat remained stock still as she bent down and picked it up. It immediately sank its teeth into the web of her thumb.

Blood welled from the bite as she returned to the others and offered the rat to them. Yendl and Haast allowed it to bite them.

'Red Haven gathered,' said Isolde.

'Red Haven confirmed,' said the rat, and expired in Haast's hands.

Yendl extended a fine cutting tool from her augmetic hand and sliced the rat from jaw to the base of its tail. Haast spread the belly. Inside, the rat was mostly cybernetic, a tiny mechanism surrounded by meat. Haast retrieved a silver ball from a housing at the centre. It bleeped, and a recorded message began to play.

'Red Haven. This is Grand Master Vangorich. I have received Yendl's troubling information regarding Kubik's new experiments. Our suspicions that he is working entirely for the good of Mars and not the Imperium as a whole are being sadly borne out. We must prepare contingencies for a final solution.

'Yendl, gather information on this new venture. Find out what the Adeptus Mechanicus want so many ork bodies for, and what they are doing with them. Prime your noospheric plague phage for release. If the Adeptus Mechanicus make their move, we shall decapitate the priesthood and destroy its informational network. Haast, hand over the care of Tybalt to Isolde. You are the most talented infiltrator in the cell. I want you to watch Kubik night and day. Build up a complete picture of his every habit. Operational level detail to be collated and submitted to me by the end of next week via the usual channels. Once you have this, Haast, you and Isolde are to find a suitable deployment site for Tybalt, and secrete him nearby. Isolde, begin preparation to infiltrate Kubik's household as soon as Haast has performed her task. I want all three of you in position. One Assassin may be stopped, four cannot be.'

'He's going to assassinate the Fabricator General of Mars? He's overstepping his office,' said Raznick. 'Can't you see that? Let me report to my superiors! If you go through with this, it will mean civil war.'

'Preparation does not betoken execution,' said Isolde. 'Preparedness is the watchword of the Officio Assassinorum.'

'We're going to have to kill you, Raznick,' said Haast.

'Your task is great, but you have my utmost confidence,' Vangorich was saying. 'The survival of the Imperium hangs by a thread. No matter your duty, I know you will perform it without question. I know you will succeed.'

'Raznick's death was the only outcome,' said Isolde. 'Did you think we might let him live, Haast?'

'No,' Haast said.

Raznick sank resignedly into the floor. 'Just make it quick,' he said.

'Of course,' said Isolde. 'Suffering in this instance is of benefit to no one.' She took a small knife from an arm sheath. Its blue steel edges began to vibrate once it was drawn. 'Present your throat,' said Isolde. 'It's the quickest way.'

'Vangorich hasn't finished yet,' said Yendl. 'Leave it.'

'Finally,' said Vangorich's recording. 'There is an Inquisitorial agent by the name of Raznick who has been assigned to follow you. If you have not already killed him, do not harm him. Make contact with him. It is in the interests of the Imperium that the Inquisition and Officio Assassinorum work together. Inquisitorial Representative Veritus has placed the Inquisition's assets on Mars at our disposal. Raznick is the key to them.'

Isolde bent down to Raznick and cut his bonds. The ties offered no more resistance to the blade than smoke. He sat up and rubbed his wrists.

'Today is my lucky day,' he said.

'Good hunting, Red Haven,' concluded Vangorich.

Haast dropped the ball. It hit the plascrete. She stamped on it hard, breaking it into pieces.

'Well then, my ladies,' said Raznick from the floor, 'what is our next move?'

NINETEEN

Witch

In tight formation, the *Palimodes* and the *Obsidian Sky* drove through the ork fleet, brothers once more, if but for a while. Ramshackle ork craft were blasted apart at close quarters by punishing broadsides issuing from the ships. Spinal lances stabbed out, vaporising smaller craft and raking long, glowing rents into the sides of the others.

On the command deck of the *Obsidian Sky*, the Black Templars bondsmen went about their duties efficiently. Ericus sat tensely in his command throne, reading the ebb and flow of battle through augur and implant. '*Palimodes*, you are drifting ahead,' said Ericus. 'Maintain formation for maximum concentration of fire.'

Attonax responded, vox only, his voice crackling as much with anger as the constant, thumping roar of the orks' broadsides. 'I am not yours to command.'

'If you wish to see your master returned to your vessel, you are,' said Ericus. 'By all means, we can go back to our previous bellicosity instead if you wish. If not, regain formation.'

The *Palimodes* slipped back, rolling a few degrees as attitude jets adjusted its trim.

'That's better,' said Ericus to himself. 'Proceed forward,' he ordered. 'We're close to breaking out of this.'

A flight of ork attack craft swooped down for an attack run on the prow of the ship, guns spitting. A storm of anti-fighter fire tore them apart. The *Obsidian Sky* rocked as a massive projectile impacted on the void shields, overloading a power conduit high up in the command deck's ceiling. Sparks showered down.

'Master Scutum, report!'

'Port void shield is down.'

'Get it up. Intensify port fire. They've barely scratched us, we'll make it through. Twelve degrees to port, helm, steady adjustment. Get me a good line on the target. *Palimodes*, prepare for synchronised fire.'

'As you say, shipmaster,' responded a surly Attonax.

The last obstacle in their path tracked across the hololith with the *Obsidian Sky*'s course adjustment, an ugly brute of a ship created by collision rather than construction. Much of the front half was made up of a crude, toothed beak, like that of an oceanic predator. This deliberate design gave way to a humped mass of rock studded with cannons and towers. Behind that the drive section sprouted a collection of tubes jutting off in multiple directions.

'Prepare to diverge, Attonax. We'll take the underside, you the top.'

The ork ship was coming about, its mismatched engines erratically flaring.

'Too easy,' said Ericus.

An impact shivered the *Obsidian Sky*. Ericus kept his focus upon the cruiser.

'Second wave of boarders reported, teleport. Multiple contacts on seven decks.' The Master Augurum looked back to his instruments. 'I have high-energy emissions close by. They're coming for the command deck.'

Gunfire, feeble and popping compared to the thunderous rolls of the ship's main batteries, sounded from outside. Men shouted in the distance, competing with the joyous roaring of orks at war.

'Secure the deck. Close blast doors. Let free the spirits of our weapon emplacements,' commanded Ericus. Red lights spun and flashed. A harsh klaxon heralded the sealing of the command deck. 'Lord Rolans will deal with our uninvited guests. Every man aboard this deck must save his thoughts for the destruction of our target. The lives of our masters depend upon success. Do not waver from your purpose!'

The ork ship came closer, dominating the hololith. 'Open the oculus once more, let's set eyes upon the vessel. Gunnery, prepare for fire. Charge lances. Hold broadsides for passing. Attonax, *Palimodes* to perform the same, confirm.'

'As you say, Ericus. One day I will make you regret ordering me around so.'

'Perhaps you have a better plan?'

Attonax remained silent.

'All hands, prepare!' commanded Ericus.

The oculus shutters slid open. Bright planetshine chased away the dimness of the bridge. The ork ship was above them relative to the pull of the *Obsidian Sky*'s grav-plating. Its dorsal aspect faced the planet, the *Palimodes* cutting between it and the hazy caramel of Dzelenic IV's atmosphere. In life it was even uglier than upon the hololithic tactical display, a mechanical parody of a diseased void-whale, its stone and metal skin pocked by cosmic impacts, back crooked. It was far from defenceless for all its primitive construction, and a hundred guns of all sizes spat orange fire from every side.

'Prow up twelve degrees. Master Scutum, concentrate shield replenishment on prow. Gunnery, on my mark. Target amidships. Tear it in two.'

The underside of the ork ship moved down across the oculus as the *Obsidian Sky* pointed itself directly at the planetary equator. The fire from the other ork ships had slackened off, most having been destroyed, the rest fleeing in disarray.

'Fire lances!' ordered Ericus.

'Firing lances!'

Five energy beams stabbed out from the *Obsidian Sky*. The ship was still moving upwards relative to the ork cruiser, and they carved a deep wound of molten rock into the asteroid that made up the middle section of the craft. The *Palimodes* opened fire a second later. Turrets sheared off and floated away to join the debris cloud of the battle. Fire and the explosions of touched-off munitions stores burst from across the surface. The ork cruiser continued firing. *Obsidian Sky*'s forward void shield blazed and winked out, and the mass projectiles cast out by the ork ship slammed into the vessel's armour. Rumbling troubled the *Obsidian Sky*, and Ericus was obliged to shout.

'Roll to starboard, eighty degrees! Increase forward thrust. Prepare to fire starboard weapons batteries. *Palimodes*, we shall go first. Hold back, or we shall hit each other.' Only hours before, that was exactly what they had been trying to do. Now the two ships fought together as if they had been part of the same fleet for decades.

The ork ship slipped out of direct view. The surface of Dzelenic IV filled the oculus, nothing but debris from the battle between the *Obsidian Sky* and the rescue of the Marshal. Ericus watched the target upon the hololith for the perfect moment to strike.

'Fire starboard battery!' he yelled.

A ripple of shock waves shook the vessel as its main guns fired. 'Give me a visual feed!' shouted Ericus. The hololith representation was replaced by a pict feed from the starboard-side pict-eyes. Hundreds of shells slammed into the ork ship, each bursting into a perfect sphere of atomic fire. Then the *Obsidian Sky* was past. Ericus ordered a rear view projected, so that he could watch the *Palimodes*' attack run. It came in the wake of the *Obsidian Sky*, unleashing its own salvo as the fires from the first were blinking out. Another blooming of atomic destruction followed. The *Palimodes* sailed past as the ork ship broke into multiple pieces, trailing gas and corpses.

A cheer went up from the command deck. Behind the *Obsidian Sky* the ork fleet was a shattered mess of metal, stone and frozen atmosphere. The sound of fighting outside the blast doors was subsiding.

'Raise Lord Magneric and Lord Castellan Ralstan. We shall launch extraction craft as soon as they command,' said Ericus.

* * *

From every window, boltguns fired, cutting down orks by the dozen. Time after time the orks attempted the walls, only to be thrown back. Breaching teams were targeted by disciplined Space Marine fire. Heavy weapons were neutralised, tanks and guns eliminated by long-range lascannon shots. The swarms of orks hurling themselves at the walls were further thinned by grenades and careful flamer bursts. Large-calibre ork bullets took chunks from the ancient rockcrete. Rockets spiralled in on corkscrews of black smoke, leaving smoking craters in the walls, but none could penetrate the building.

'Slay them! Slay them all!' roared Magneric. Unable to go within, he stood behind a berm of rubble torn from the desert sands by the Iron Warriors. His men fired from behind him, killing those orks that posed a threat to the ancient, while Magneric himself selected targets on the basis of size. The bigger the ork, the more likely they were to receive the attentions of Magneric's assault cannon.

Within the building, Kalkator paced the buckled floors, shouting encouragement and curses at his men. Ralstan shadowed his every step, alert for treachery, but there was none. The Black Templars and Iron Warriors were thoroughly intermingled, fighting as one force. Ties to the old Legions were forgotten, treachery was put out of mind. They fought together as Space Marines, born of the same science, equipped with the same weaponry and armour. Blood and battle removed the differences between them. Ralstan's misgivings were swamped for a while by martial pride. His desire to show the Iron Warriors who were the greater warriors had him exhorting his brothers to greater accuracy, smoother fire, wiser target selection.

'Do not fear, my brothers!' he shouted. 'We shall meet them blade to blade soon enough. Kill them now at distance, lay their vile xenos hides low into the dust of this world. When they are bloodied and enraged, then shall we test ourselves against them!'

'If this were a larger force, or better equipped, we would perish here,' said Kalkator to Ralstan.

'Maybe you would. The Black Templars will not be bested!'

'A larger ork attack annihilated two of my worlds,' said Kalkator, 'and reduced my Great Company to this sad remnant. You speak from ignorance. You would have died.'

'Never!' said Ralstan. 'Not while the Emperor watches over us.' He left Kalkator, irked by his sniping, and went up onto the roof. Joy at battle filled him. Afterwards, he would have more words with the Marshal about disobeying the call to the Last Wall, but for now the reality of battle was a clean wind, scouring his soul and his thoughts of doubt. If they could not battle the orks with the rest of their Chapter, so be it. Here was the chance of great slaughter!

He looked out over the ork horde. There were thousands of them, but there was some truth to what Kalkator said. These were pirates, opportunists ranging ahead of the main fleets. They had little heavy equipment, and their fleet was locked in battle with the *Palimodes* and the *Obsidian Sky*. If there were an attack moon, the situation would be different. A scouting group, he thought. And still there were five thousand orks and more.

A bright flash drew his eyes heavenward. Night brought no thinning of the dust clouds that hid the face of Dzelenic IV, but when the sun had gone the weapons discharge of the void battle raging overhead replaced its light.

'Ship death,' said Ralstan.

The vox hissed in his ear.

'Castellan Ralstan, Marshal Magneric, respond. This is the *Obsidian Sky.*'

'Castellan Ralstan responding, shipmaster.'

'Yes, my lord.' Ericus sounded exulted, pleased. Ralstan heard victory in his voice. 'The ork fleet is shattered. We are free and able to bring you back aboard. Is this your desire?'

Ralstan wanted to say no. Every warrior's instinct told him to remain and slay until no ork breathed upon Dzelenic IV. With difficulty, he replied. 'Begin extraction immediately. We are surrounded by orks. Extend air cover to the Iron Warriors gunships. Escort them down.'

'My lord?'

'An oath was taken,' said Ralstan.

'Thunderhawks are away,' said Ericus. 'Prepare for evacuation.'

Ralstan watched the sky. In twenty minutes gunships would come screaming from orbit, scouring the orks from the building. Then one short flight awaited.

After that, they could drop this pretence at alliance.

A change came over the orks. Their cries of frustration became barbarous cheers, starting in the east, running out until all the filthy masses of them cried and beat their chests. Ralstan hurried over to the east corner of the building. There, at the back of the ork force, shone a sickly light in the dark. A hush fell over the orks. At some signal invisible to Ralstan, the xenos drew back from the building, leaving a wide area free of everything but their dead.

A familiar pressure troubled his skull. Thunder cracked in the distance.

'Witch!' he spat in disgust.

The psyker came escorted by burly orks in heavy armour. A dozen more scrawny examples capered and danced behind him. The witch was peculiar in appearance, even for an ork, carrying no gun or heavy cutting blade, only a long copper staff chained to his wrist in a manner similar to the oath bonds of the Black Templars' weapons. Upon his chest hung a breastplate of ribs strung together. Bone fetishes and shiny scraps of metal dangled from his tusks and ears. He wore a huge greatcoat, filched from an ogryn by the looks of it. He was wholly incongruous, a whimsical creature in marked contrast to the brutal practicality of the other orks, but that he was a being of great power was not in doubt. A nimbus of green energy haloed his head. Fizzing sparks spat from his mouth when he roared, sending his insane followers into paroxysms of laughter.

The orks parted to let him through, and he strode forward, twitching and cackling, his massive minders gimlet-eyed by his sides.

Magneric reset his ocular magnification to standard.

Through his vox-link, Magneric listened to his castellan confer with Kalkator. 'Have your men take it down,' said Ralstan.

'I have already commanded them to do so.'

'Lascannons will do no good,' interrupted Magneric.

'We shall see,' said Kalkator. 'Heavy support, open fire.'

The shot was a clear one, a straight line down an avenue

of orks directly to the psyker. Three beams of ruby light leapt down this path, aimed precisely at the ork. They struck home with terrible power, enough to cut a Land Raider in two. A second light burst from the psyker in response, meeting with that of the cannons and obscuring the witch. When it dissipated the psyker strode on, laughing madly, its dancing followers somersaulting and leaping about in ecstasy.

'Again!' snapped Kalkator.

The ork raised his hand, waved it up and down sharply. A jet of energy flicked out from it, singeing the ground. Where it rolled over dead orks they jiggled and danced, momentarily animated by the psyker's might. The jet grew broader and brighter the closer it came to the building. It made no sound as it bore down straight upon the weathered walls.

'Down, down!' yelled Ralstan. Power-armoured warriors scrambled to get out of the way as the blast hit the building. It connected silently, passing ethereally through the walls, then the ork clasped his hand and ripped it backward, and the rockcrete of the building sundered. The ruin shook with the force. Atomised rockcrete sprayed outward in a cloud. Where the energy touched Black Templar or Iron Warrior, they convulsed and fell dead. Armour collapsed, helmets rolled free, allowing the liquid remains to pour onto the ground. In a second, the dynamic of the battle changed. The walls were breached, the way was open to the orks.

They heard the indrawing of breath coming from the horde.

'Waaagh!' they bellowed. 'WAAAAAAAAAAGHHHHHH!' The orks broke into a run, coming at the hole in the wall, heedless of the hundreds felled by booming boltguns.

'We cannot hold this building,' voxed Magneric. 'We must attack. If their witch falls, they may withdraw. It is our only chance of survival.'

'We will be slaughtered,' said Kalkator. 'We must only hold out for another handful of minutes.'

'We will be dead. The gunships downed. The witch must die.'

'Then we shall fight with you, Magneric. In honour of the times before,' said Kalkator.

'No,' said Magneric, stepping over the low wall of his emplacement. The orks were only fifty metres away, and coming in fast from all sides. 'There is one defence proof against this sorcery, and that is faith,' said Magneric. 'Black Templars, to me!'

The Black Templars abandoned their positions by the Iron Warriors, leaping from windows and rooftop, rushing to join their Marshal.

'Cover us,' said Ralstan to Kalkator, jumping outside, his armour absorbing the shock of the six-metre drop.

'Iron Warriors!' shouted Kalkator. 'To the breach! Clear the way for the Black Templars, or we shall all perish.'

TWENTY

Faith and iron

The Black Templars lined up on either side of their Marshal, already firing. Sword Brethren ran to form an escort around him.

The orks closed. Flamers sang their deadly song of fire, incinerating dozens. Several came through, skin blazing, still ready to fight. These were felled by shots from the building, or died upon the waiting swords of the Templars. When a space was cleared the Black Templars opened fire again with long-practised discipline, rapid bursts of mass-reactives that together made an impenetrable wall.

Magneric lifted up his vox-amplifiers to their maximum. 'Let none survive! Destroy them all! He that feareth the witch has conceded defeat, even as his boltgun sings still in his hand! Attack, attack!'

The Dreadnought led from the front, his assault cannon blazing. At a run he slammed into the press of orks, smiting them with his power fist. His assault cannon glowed hot, blazing through the last few thousand rounds in a glorious

sheet of searing death, felling orks in a wide swathe. Those closest to the rotating barrels of the cannon were blasted apart, a fine mist of flesh and blood bursting from them. As far as forty metres from the Dreadnought, orks were torn to pieces, limbs and heads scattering.

Sweeping back and forth, Magneric carved a bloody road to the ork psyker. The fire of his Black Templars and the Iron Warriors in the building behind him kept them from surging back in. Behind him his men advanced, firing relentlessly. Magneric made straight for the witch, bashing any greenskin that came between them off its feet, lofting them high over the heads of the others. His last rounds cut down the creature's bodyguard, but no more. Bullets sent true at the witch were deflected as the las-cannons had been, or exploded with bright, green flashes. The psyker gibbered and pranced, waving its copper staff above its head in challenge. Its lunatic entourage ran past him, fingers hooked to tear at the Dreadnought. From behind, a trio of crude walkers waddled up to intercept the Marshal.

Magneric's assault cannon ceased firing. Warning chimes sang in his sensorium – ammunition depleted. The five-digit counter for the weapon's rounds glowed red: five large zeroes.

'Thou shalt not escape my wrath!' roared Magneric, and pressed forward. Orks surged in to fill the gap, readily as water flooding back. But Magneric was already moving, his short legs pumping, shifting the great bulk of his armoured tomb into an unstoppable run. Orks were barged aside by his mass, slammed to paste under his armoured tread. The biggest of them were flung away, bones shattered. Nothing could stop him.

Behind Magneric the brothers of the Black Templars continued their advance. Ordinarily guarded in their new faith, they sang their hymns to the Emperor openly, chanting prayers never heard upon the lips of a Space Marine. Flamers sent out rolling clouds of white-hot promethium, melting the orks by the score as they sought to regain lost ground. Where they passed between the cones of fire, they were met by bolts that slew and maimed. The press of greenskins was so great that the Templars could not keep them back forever, but they had no intention of doing so. This was a prelude to the real struggle. The rage of Dorn burned hot in them. Let their brother Chapters plan and fortify. That was not their way.

'Sigismund!' they shouted. 'For the glory of the black cross! For the Emperor, holy Lord of Terra! Praise be!'

Five rounds of disciplined fire, and they let out a deafening war cry. 'No fear, no regret, no mercy!' They drew their chainswords and axes and charged, singing glories to the Emperor as they ran, surging past Magneric into the horde of orks.

Deep within the crowding adamantium of his towering tomb, the hearts of Magneric lifted at what he witnessed. He pressed on, Sword Brethren to his left and right. Volleys of bolter fire punched orks from their feet. The greenskins beat around him, unstoppable as the sea. He was a rock, and their fury was spent harmlessly on the metal of his skin. The Templars clove through them swiftly and surely, men o'war defying the tempest.

'The Emperor protects!' boomed Magneric. His storm bolter chattered its approval of his piety. 'Blessed be the Lord of Mankind! Lift up your spirits, my brothers. Regard that which is true and eternal. Praise be to the God-Emperor, praise be to the saviour of humanity! Praise be! Praise be! Praise be!'

'Praise be!' scores of voices shouted back.

Strange lightnings crackled around the forces of the orks. Writhing bolts of power leapt skyward, punching rippled holes in the clouds. Tendrils of energy rose from the green-skins' heavy faces, the fury of their vile breed feeding the powers of their sorcerer. Screaming curses, the weirdboy swept down his staff, and a beam of green warpfire vomited from his mouth, incinerating the orks that stood between the witch and the Dreadnought. No machine nor man could stand up to such raw power, and the weirdboy cackled through the fires at the doom his gods had unleashed upon his enemy. But the green fire hit an invisible barrier, splashing outwards in a writhing of broken might. The Dreadnought was unharmed.

'I do not fear you!' roared Magneric. 'For the Emperor guides my right hand! His regard is ever on me, and His glory cloaks me. Behold the radiant might of the Lord of Terra! Behold the power of His champion! Abhor the witch, deny the witch, destroy the witch!'

'Praise be!' shouted the Black Templars.

The weirdboy shrank backwards. He lifted his hands to the air, calling up a storm of eldritch power from the warriors around him. Spectral light brought an early dawn to the battlefield, greenish and sinister, a howling maelstrom building that tugged ork wraithforms partially free of their bodies, hungry for their souls. The orks howled the louder, and began to chant. 'Gork! Mork! Gork! Mork! Gork! Mork!' a guttural rumbling that grew faster and faster until the names blurred into one. 'Gorkamorkagorkamorkagorkamorka!'

The psyker was only metres in front of Magneric, arms held to the sky, his demented face lit by blazing white-green power. A whirlwind of abominable psychic energy raced around and around him, sparks of it spearing from his eyes, ears and mouth.

One of Magneric's attendant Sword Brethren was cut down by his foes, his sword arm grabbed, bolter torn from his hand, his helm wrenched from his head. Another disappeared into a firefly swarm of sparks, disintegrated by a bizarre energy weapon. The others found themselves surrounded, and fought back to back. Their line was disrupted, leaving Magneric to go on alone.

The three walkers moved in front of Magneric as he closed upon his target. The first died, its cylindrical pilot's compartment crushed by a single swing of Magneric's four-fingered power fist. Magneric barged its remains aside, spraying lubricant and blood. The second swiped at him with cruel shears, grabbing at the stilled barrels of his assault cannon. The blades squealed on metal. Magneric wrenched himself free, rotating his torso to slam his fist again and again into the smaller walker. On the fourth strike, its primitive power plant detonated. Magneric stepped through a roiling cloud of fire to see the last machine stumbling away. He let it go. The psyker was before him.

'Gorkamorkagorkamorkagorkamorka!' chanted the orks.

The psyker's power drove them into a frenzy, and they hewed and cut and threw themselves again and again at the Black Templars, dragging many to their dooms.

'This ends now,' said Magneric. 'O Emperor of Terra, lord of the stars! Once more cast Your protection about me, so that I might slay this enemy of Yours.'

'Praise be!' answered the Black Templars. They were few, but the strength of their faith made them sound legion.

He strode forward. A beam of light blazed from the psyker's eyes, splashing to nothing before it could touch Magneric. The Marshal leaned forward, grabbing the weird-boy's head. Energy leapt uncontrollably from the thing's cranium, earthing itself in his armour.

'So perish all unclean witches,' said Magneric, and shut his fist, crushing the ork's skull.

The vortex about the ork burst outward at the moment of its death, slamming into Magneric with such force that he came close to toppling backward. Green lines of power stabbed out, spearing orks.

And the orks died.

They fell by the hundred, heads exploded by psychic feedback, or their souls torn from their bodies. They dropped as the shock wave raced over them. Walkers clanked to a halt. Vehicles ran out of control or skidded and toppled over.

The light dissipated. Lightning chased itself across the skies.

Magneric turned from side to side. Half of his warriors were dead; the rest stood in a sea of corpses, black armour battered, scrips and robes bloody, but alive nonetheless. There was not a single ork left standing on the battlefield.

'The witches,' rumbled Magneric, and his voice was as thunder upon the suddenly silent field. 'Their witches are their weakness! My brothers, the Emperor shows us the way! He delivers us victory, and in His beneficence reveals the road to final triumph! This is why we were sent here, this is why He brought us to Dzelenic Four. Praise be!'

As one, the Black Templars got to their knees, clasped their hands about the hilts of the swords, drove the points into the earth and bowed their heads.

'Praise be!' they shouted, and the faith in them burned twice as bright at their deliverance.

Kalkator took refuge from the energy wave as it hit the building. When it passed he stood, and to his amazement found himself looking down upon a field of dead orks. The Dreadnought marched across the corpses towards the fort, bellowing pieties, surrounded by his warriors singing hymns for the Emperor. Magneric stopped below the walls and angled his glacis upward.

'What is this?' said Kalkator. 'The cult of the Emperor as god has grown so strong it has you in its clutches?'

'What of it? I will not deny my faith! See, warsmith.' Magneric raised a mighty metal fist and rotated upon his waist gimbal, showing the devastation of the battlefield triumphantly. 'How can you deny it? You have witnessed the glory of the Emperor first hand, and that the strength of the Emperor is paramount over all things! Even sorely wounded upon His Golden Throne, He wields a power that cannot be denied! Nothing can stop Him, nor those who serve Him truly with faith within their hearts. One day He will rid the galaxy of all evil, for unlike the creatures you threw your lot in with He is just. Justice comes for you, Kalkator, the Emperor's justice, and all your wicked betrayers will be destroyed for your treachery. Look upon this battlefield, look upon the slaughter. This was done by His will alone. That is why we follow Him.'

Kalkator gripped at the parapet, looking down on the enemy who, so long ago, had been a friend.

'I am genuinely at a loss for words. Do your loyalist brothers know you have caught the madness of the puling herds and have turned your back upon the Imperial Truth, the lie you fought so hard to protect? That you are casting it aside for the greatest heresy of all?'

'The Emperor protected us with His lie,' said Kalkator. 'He protected us further by denying His godhood. We have had the scales lifted from our eyes. He is a god. The proof is around us everywhere, here on this battleground.'

Lights appeared in the sky, growing brighter. The Thunderhawks were coming.

'You are abandoning everything you vowed to honour, and you call me a traitor?' said Kalkator. 'Such irony is a rare thing, Magneric. Do all your warriors follow this insane creed?'

'Each and every one,' said Magneric proudly.

'Then you are treading the same deluded path as Lorgar. How will the other Space Marines look upon this great naiveté? Common humanity already worships the Emperor, and I say again, against His express wishes. All that is, Magneric, is an expression of their weakness and desire to be dominated, and proof of the Emperor's desire to be worshipped despite His protestations. It appears Lorgar was but a little too early with his devotion. What would your Emperor make of you now? Would He hold out a hand for you to kiss while you grovel upon your knees? Or would He smash your face in with a mailed fist as He did to Lorgar?'

'We would take either gladly,' said Magneric, 'if it meant our Lord would walk among men once more.'

Engine noise rumbled. The extraction craft approached, seven of them, and began to set down one after the other in the wreckage of the field. Kalkator's Thunderhawks opened their hatches, and his men began to leave the building. The Black Templars made no move to stop them. They remained kneeling, heads bowed in prayer as the Iron Warriors passed between them.

'Such devotion. Perhaps the Emperor is a god, after all, if He can inspire sane men to worship Him so,' said Kalkator.

'Embrace this truth, and your soul will be saved!' said Magneric eagerly.

Kalkator laughed. Before he left the roof to join his warriors aboard their craft, he shouted down to Magneric. 'I am not going to convert to your pathetic creed, Magneric. For if I cannot trust a man who lies, I trust a god who does so even less.'

Ralstan came to Magneric's side, his wargear dripping gore. Kalkator's gunships were taking off and heading for the sky. The Black Templars were preparing to leave, honouring their dead with silent prayer as they gathered up the wargear of the fallen and extracted gene-seed to safeguard against the future.

'We could order them shot down as soon as they break atmosphere,' said the castellan.

Magneric's torso tilted backwards, watching the Iron Warriors gunships recede, becoming glowing balls of fire rising high into the night.

'No. Let the hunt begin anew. We honour the oaths we make in battle, castellan, or we are no better than they.'

TWENTY-ONE

Three partings

Kubik arrived in the temple of the diagnostic covens as the interrogation was ending. In a chamber deep underground, the dead Assassin was suspended from the ceiling, hands and feet fully enclosed in manacles. Portions of her skin had been removed, exposing bloodless muscles. Spaces in her anatomy hinted at the devices removed from her body. A domed helmet enclosed her head, studded all over with conical spikes from which curled multiple silver wires.

A lone genetor interogatis worked the machines probing the dead Assassin's brain, accompanied by coil-handed servitors whose sole purpose was to adjust the magnetism of two tall field modulators.

'Ah, Fabricator General, you arrive in time for the climax of my investigation. Most of the information I have extracted has been through the memorandum parsers. It should be ready soon. Bear with me as I finish this final interrogation.'

The genetor was a repulsive thing, a skinny flesh torso supported on limbs of slender sliding rods. His voice was papery, eager. He was a man who enjoyed his repellent work. 'One moment, and I shall have the information you desire.' He returned to his howling machines.

Kubik waited behind a buffering screen, lest his own bioelectrical field destroy the data being culled from the woman's memory. He did not have to remain there for long. The machines cut out. A wet crack preceded the withdrawal of the helmet from the woman's head. Wormy cyber-tentacles wriggled from her skull, dripping matter. The corpse shuddered.

'I have all the raw data,' said the genetor interogatis. 'It will take a little while to transpose the last few fragments into binharic instructions my cogitators might process, and thence to image and sound...' The genetor trailed off, absorbed in his task. Kubik waited twelve minutes. 'There, I have it.'

'Show me,' said Kubik.

'The image quality will be lacking, Fabricator General,' said the genetor apologetically. 'The woman was fresh, but draw-ing information from an unmodified brain is always the hardest. Editicore processors are the best, but even the least intelligence core can offer up a mind's secrets. Alas, here we must rely on the primitive wiring of the flesh.'

He threw a lever with one three-fingered metal hand. An elliptical screen flickered on the wall.

'There. The most recent memory I could recover, and I believe the most relevant. To go through her entire life will take time, even those few fragments that survived her death. But I think this will be helpful, great prime.'

Kubik ignored the prattling of the genetor, and watched

the picts run, a jumble of images in no particular order. A lesser mind would have made no sense of them, but Kubik's augmetics automatically recorded the images, and began to re-edit them into something approaching usability. He watched a scene from a few days ago, the gathering of an Assassin cadre. They stood around the loading ramp of an automated haulage barge in an obscure section of the Olympian landing fields. Where exactly, Kubik could not tell. There were five of them. The dead girl, three more on foot, one in a cryo-containment unit. Kubik seethed to see them meeting in the shadow of his own seat of power. The images jumped, running out of sequence, the scene changing to the vagaries of imperfect human recollection.

Four Assassins remained at liberty. Five was an unusually high number for one cell. Kubik had sat in the Senatorum for hundreds of years and had been involved in the authorisation votes for several high-level assassinations. One Assassin could topple the government of a world. But five? Deployment of such a number within the Imperium was reserved for the holders of the very highest offices, those who could call upon substantial resources – rogue admirals, corrupt cardinals, the renegade lords of star systems, or perhaps even a High Lord of Terra...

Kubik appraised the images, using what little he knew of the Officio Assassinorum to fit the operatives with the temples. The metronomic tick of his augmetic regulators stuttered when he identified the Eversor Temple adept within the cryo-containment pod, a creature so violent it had to be kept in suspended animation.

A further jumble of images showed him Vangorich on

the ramp of the ship. Vangorich had been on Mars – he had come to Mars on one of Kubik's own vessels! Kubik's anger rose. The cell had been deployed by his direct order. This was no routine mission.

The images played one last time, and faded out.

'That is the extent of it, my lord. There is no more,' said the genetor.

'Your efforts are noted,' said Kubik, and departed the chamber without further word. He had seen enough.

Five Assassins. There could be only one explanation. One reason to deploy such a powerful cadre on Mars. Was there not only one target of sufficient power and value? Only one so well protected that five of the most deadly killers in the galaxy would be required to ensure certain death?

Himself.

Vangorich intended to kill *him*.

The auditorium seemed bigger than ever to Mesring. The masses of worshippers within the nave of the vast subterranean cathedral seemed to stretch away into infinity, a sea of hopeless souls beseeching him for salvation. Vat-cherubs and psyber-birds jostled for space with servo-skulls in the incense-choked air. The breathing of the crowd was a soft wind.

Mesring was sweating long before the sermon was done. The free-floating vox-horns and vox-pieces on ornate stands crowded in on him. He stumbled through his second homily, cutting short the service with a hurried blessing when his tongue thickened and stuck in his mouth halfway through the third.

The ranks of cardinals at the back of Auditorium Oratio stage stared as he lurched past them.

'Your holiness?' one asked.

He ignored her, banging through the doors, his Frateris Templar guard catching him before he ploughed into the corridor wall opposite. Head spinning, he left the Auditorium Oratio and blundered along thick carpets towards his private exit. By the time he had left the Basilica Vox Imperatorum, he had difficulty walking, staggering past his sedan chair and the waiting servitors. Three lesser priests gently turned him around and put him inside. The box lurched as the servitor bearers engaged their wheels, carrying him swiftly down the five-kilometre corridor to his private apartments. His Frateris Templars fell in beside the chair, running alongside in escort.

The sedan took him deep into the heartlands of the Ecclesiarchal hive, up long ramps to the side of the mountainous staircases leading to his palace. It drew to a halt outside the main gates in anticipation of his dismounting, but the Frateris Templar runners shouted to the guard, 'Open the gates! Open the gates! The Ecclesiarch is taken ill!'

The sedan rolled on, into the entrance hall, lofty as any cardinal world's cathedral. The crowd of sextons, servants, vergers, ushers and savants parted in confusion as the chair rolled through them, interrupting the nightly ritual of the Ecclesiarch's retiring. The vestal choirs on the stairs sang on, but their efforts were unappreciated, the sedan whisking past them swiftly.

'The Ecclesiarch is unwell!' called the Templars going before it. 'Make way, make way!' Murmurs of consternation went through the army of holy men and women waiting upon their lord.

The chair rushed along lengthy galleries to Mesring's private chambers. Outside doors clad in gold his guards helped him from the chair. He pushed them away, nearly falling inside as the doors were opened for him.

'Call for the medicae!' shouted the Templar's prior. 'We shall have a healer with you soon, my lord. For the Emperor's sake, get him to his bed.'

'No, no,' mumbled Mesring. 'No medicae or hospitaller. It will pass, it will pass.'

'Your holiness–'

'I said no healers!' he yelled. A stinking belch followed, half retch. 'It will pass. Rest, rest, I need rest.' He summoned enough strength to waver inside. 'Leave me!' he shouted to the gaggle of savant priests awaiting his return. Mesring tore at his heavy robes, ripping his cloak and mitre off, throwing them on the floor without a care. 'Hot, hot! Too damn hot!' he bellowed as he yanked madly at the multiple layers of his liturgical dress. Priests hurried to his side to aid him, and he slapped one down as he reached to undo the laces of his vestment, sending him reeling. 'Leave me be!' he spluttered.

His violent staggering had the acolytes sent to attend on him retreating with fear. With the strength of desperation, he ripped his vestments, scattering a planetary lord's ransom in jewels across the floor. His priests scurried to retrieve them.

'Out, out! Get out!' he shouted. His throat was thick with phlegm, voice clotted. He could not think, he could not stand. He staggered on through his fleeing servants, wrenching his surplice over his head, throttling himself with its laces. Nearly naked, still he was too hot!

He came to his bedchamber, and shouldered the doors open. Food had been left out for him, a tall ewer of wine, all the plate of gold and platinum. He crashed into the table, sending delicacies over the carpet. 'Where is it?' he said. 'Where is it?' He trailed off into tears, and sank to his knees into the wet mess of his dinner, weeping freely.

He stopped. An awful voice whispered to him from the covered gallery running around the walls where, for a hefty sum, the most pious lords and ladies might watch Mesring's ceremonial rising in the morning. When he peeked over the tips of his fingers, seeking it out, the statues of the stonework shifted and leered at him, shaking their heads in disapproval.

'I'm not drunk, I'm not drunk, damn you! How dare you judge me, so-called saints! No man is perfect. Am I not but a man? You sit there on your lofty walls, dead and gone, safe in the Emperor's light. It is I who must endure this world of pain and perfidy, where every smile hides a sharp tooth eager for blood, every promise is a lie. I am poisoned by Vangorich! Manipulated by Wienand. Emperor save me. Damn you, Vangorich! Emperor cast you into the warp! I... I...' He shook his head in confusion, got to his feet where he stood swaying, peering at the mess he had made.

'Why, what happened, what happened? The antidote, the antidote. I must have it. Yes, that is why I am here.' He swung around, his arms flying out from his sides, lumbering to a richly carved *Lectitio Divinatus* box on an ancient dresser. His extremities tingled painfully, and an awful burning had set up in his stomach. With numb fingers he pawed at the box catch, opening it on the fourth try. He began to cry again as he fished out a smaller box hidden inside – the jewelled skull of a holy innocent.

At the bottom of the skull box were a half-dozen tiny crystals. He tipped the box up, spilled half. Wailing loudly, he dabbed at the carpet with a wet finger, desperate to recover his treasure. He sucked his finger. The crystal dissolved, flooding his mouth with a vile acid taste that made his stomach roil, but the unpleasantness was passing, and was followed by blessed relief. He leaned against the dark wood of the dresser as first his queasiness subsided, then the spinning in his head. Relief spread out to his fingers, the numbness and pain seeping from him.

He sat slumped for some time, before recovering himself. Groaning, he got up. His room was a catastrophe. In his hand rested the small box. With woozy eyes he focused on it. There were five crystals left inside. Each dose was good for five days, five times five was twenty-five. Such a simple calculation to count out a man's life! Wienand was dead. His chances of getting more antidote were remote. He could tell no one, not without seriously compromising his position. Who would have faith in him if he were revealed to be so fallible?

Lucidity was fleeting. The poison would start its work again soon enough, and he was gripped by anxiety. He looked up to the many faces of the Emperor carved into rare woods in the friezes of his room.

'Where are You? Why don't You help me?' he whispered.

'Have I not served You faithfully? Put forward the interests of Your church where I could? So if I took a little pleasure for myself, it is nothing to the work I have done for You!' He got onto his knees and lifted a hand, clawed as if it gripped his heart and he would offer it to his god. 'Help me!'

The Emperor, His face so placid and commanding, looked everywhere but at Mesring. He gazed upon scenes from the past so distant no one could name them any more, a dead god unaware of His own irrelevance, dwelling on glories that would never be seen again.

A sharp pain stabbed through Mesring's head. 'You are weak! Self-absorbed! You denied Your godhood to the people who loved You, You used us, You use us still!' His eyes strayed eastward, and he cringed in the direction of the great dome of the Throne Room. When no reprisal came he huffed in contempt. 'But the orks, the orks!' He lifted a finger skyward. 'They are above Your Palace, and You do nothing! Why do You not smite them from the sky?'

A jangle of phantom noise shattered his thoughts. He blinked at the swaying images crowding his thoughts, his fellows gathered around his bed, jeering at him. The antidote had yet to complete its work.

'It is because the Beast is stronger than You!' he shouted.

Mesring got to his feet, and casting accusing looks over his shoulder, he went to the window of his chamber, flinging shutters wide that had remained closed for years. Acrid air flooded in. The Imperial Palace was a sea of lights shoaled by spires of metal and stone. Two moons shone down on it. Full of fear, he lifted his eyes heavenward. The ork moon's brutal face stared down at him. Mesring met its gaze. The

attack moon was surrounded by the pinprick lights of the Space Marine fleet. Surrounded by the mightiest warriors in the Imperium, and still it shone! He feared its great strength.

Strength. Undeniable, present, immanent, so unlike his deaf god.

There was something worthy of his respect.

Koorland waited to meet Thane alone in a minor shuttle bay of the *Abhorrence*. He stayed out of sight, watching Thane's bondsmen go over their small craft. Vapour curled from its engines as the pilot put them through their pre-flight warm-up, while two others went over it carefully, checking its surface and various devices inside and out. There were so many tasks the servants of a Chapter performed. They were invisible most of the time, but without them the Space Marines would not be able to function. If he were truly the Master of a Chapter, he would have to acquaint himself with their activities to a level he had never considered before.

The lord of the Fists Exemplar entered the hangar flanked by two of his honour guard. They reacted quickly when Koorland stepped out of the shadows, training their bolt-guns upon him.

'Koorland?' said Thane. 'What are you doing skulking about down here?'

'I wished to speak with you before you departed. Privately.'

Thane looked over his shoulder at his men and nodded to them. They lowered their weapons and went into the waiting vessel.

'What do you need to say to me that could not be said in front of the others?' said Thane.

'Nothing of great import,' said Koorland. 'I wanted to wish you well. You and I are in a similar position, both of us elevated to Chapter Mastery by the deaths of others.'

'Your tragedy is greater than mine, brother,' said Thane. 'My Chapter survives.'

'As does mine, so long as I live. I must use however much time is left to me well.'

'A noble aim, brother,' said Thane.

'I wanted to impress upon you a need for great care. Not against the orks, but against hubris. Issachar is agitating that we should go further. The Last Wall has shown the efficacy of a large force of Space Marines gathered together. He has not done so yet, but it will not be long before he openly advocates the reformation of the Legion. I know you are sympathetic to his opinion. You must reconsider.'

'I see it coming,' Thane agreed. 'Our own gene-father was against the division originally. He relented only to prevent further civil strife in the Imperium.' He paused. 'What if Lord Dorn were right all along? Perhaps Lord Guilliman was the one who was wrong. What if he divided the Legions in a panic, and it has been to the detriment of the Imperium ever since?'

'A primarch does not panic.'

'How can you be sure?' said Thane. 'They are all gone.'

'We cannot countenance such a move,' said Koorland.

'Nevertheless, Issachar makes a compelling case,' said Thane. 'With our resources pooled, we can expand our numbers, bring the old Seventh to life in full, not this shadow. There are thousands of us here, but we are less than three hundredths of the full might of Dorn's original

Legion. Imagine what we could accomplish with ten thousand, fifty thousand, even a hundred thousand warriors? This entire war with the orks would never have arisen in the first place, but been crushed before it even began.'

'That is exactly why Roboute Guilliman split the Legions. His foresight was great. Such power in the hands of one man, no matter how well intentioned, is dangerous. Our actions would undoubtedly start purely, but how many wrong decisions would it take for our successors to go astray, not realising their mistakes until it is too late and the Imperium once more burns in the fire of schism? The primarchs themselves did not manage to avoid that path. We will become tyrants, no matter our desire. The High Lords were put in place by the Emperor. We have no right to defy His wishes.'

'That is the propaganda of the High Lords.'

'It is the truth,' said Koorland.

Thane exhaled heavily. 'Then something must be done to return them to their original purpose. They are ineffective, divided. Their intrigues have brought the Imperium to its knees.'

'Listen to the discussions between we Chapter Masters, who are brothers. Are we any different? We work in concert now, but already disagreement is on the horizon. I agree, something needs to be done. I will not bow to Udo's demands and split the fleet before this crisis is resolved, but once it is, we must set the Senatorum in order, and go our separate ways.'

Thane thought a moment. 'Maybe you are right. Power is seductive.'

'Before that comes to pass, we have much to do. Udo

presents us with a problem. Your departure will allay his fears for a while, but we must be prepared for strong resistance when you return. An increase in our numbers will anger him.'

'I do not envy you, re-entering that snake pit.'

'I am learning. Gather our brothers. I will deal with the High Lords. Find the Soul Drinkers, Brother Thane. Take our tidings to every Chapter that will listen, but when you return, do so in good conscience,' said Koorland. 'The Emperor set us above men, but He never intended us to rule over them. The moment we forget that, the Imperium is doomed.'

Thane and Koorland clasped arms, true brothers in every sense.

'I will do as you suggest, Slaughter,' Thane said, using Koorland's wall-name. 'You have proven yourself worthy of your office. There is wisdom in you. I will think on you often, brother, and hope it is not tested too sorely.'

Thane went to his shuttle. Koorland watched as the craft's engines built to a throaty roar and it took off on four columns of fire. Angling its propulsion units backward, the shuttle sailed out of the hangar, through the integrity field, and into space.

Bells pinged. Servitors came out of their coffins to make the hangar good again, waving the nozzles of suppressant units about them in search of non-existent fires. Their limited awareness satisfied, they clomped back to their alcoves, leaving two others to buff the scorch marks from the decking. There was none of the bustle of the embarkation decks and major docks in the bay. Surrounded by the living corpses of the servitors, to Koorland it felt like a morgue.

He walked over to the hangar slot, and stood upon the edge of space. All around Terra sailed the Space Marine armada. Naval ships had been joining them daily, the mighty *Autocephalax Eternal*, that had so cravenly held back from their assault, sailing proudly at their head. At the centre of the blockade, circled by vigilant frigates and destroyers, the ork moon hung balefully, the great insult to Terra.

Koorland stared at the moon. The insults would keep coming from all quarters. Soon Udin Macht Udo would demand the Space Marines fleet redeploy. To defy the Lord Guilliman might well be as foolish as to cast himself through the field. Koorland looked down past his feet, past the lip of the hangar bay, into the yawning depths of space.

Sometimes, he thought, victory requires a leap of faith.

ABOUT THE AUTHOR

Guy Haley is the author of the Space Marine Battles novel *Death of Integrity*, the Warhammer 40,000 novels *Valedor* and *Baneblade*, and the novellas *The Eternal Crusader*, *The Last Days of Ector* and *Broken Sword*, for *Damocles*. His enthusiasm for all things greenskin has also led him to pen the eponymous Warhammer novel *Skarsnik*, as well as the End Times novel *The Rise of the Horned Rat*. He lives in Yorkshire with his wife and son.

The Beast Arises continues in Book VI

Echoes of the Long War
by David Guymer

May 2016

Available from
blacklibrary.com and